Women

Women

Chloe Caldwell

4th ESTATE • *London*

4th Estate
An imprint of HarperCollins*Publishers*
1 London Bridge Street
London SE1 9GF

www.4thEstate.co.uk

First published in Great Britain in 2018 by 4th Estate

First published in the United States by Short Flight/Long Drive Books
a division of Hobart in 2014

1

Copyright © Chloe Caldwell 2014

Chloe Caldwell asserts the moral right to be identified
as the author of this work in accordance with the
Copyright, Designs and Patents Act 1988

A catalogue record for this book is
available from the British Library

ISBN 978-0-00-825491-9

This novella is entirely a work of fiction. The names, characters
and incidents portrayed in it are the work of the author's imagination.
Any resemblance to actual persons, living or dead, events or
localities is entirely coincidental.

All rights reserved. No part of this publication may be
reproduced, stored in a retrieval system, or transmitted,
in any form or by any means, electronic, mechanical,
photocopying, recording or otherwise, without the
prior permission of the publishers.

This book is sold subject to the condition that it shall not, by
way of trade or otherwise, be lent, re-sold, hired out or otherwise
circulated without the publisher's prior consent in any form of
binding or cover other than that in which it is published and
without a similar condition including this condition being
imposed on the subsequent purchaser.

Printed and bound in Great Britain by
CPI Group (UK) Ltd, Croydon CR0 4YY

MIX
Paper from
responsible sources
FSC® C007454

This book is produced from independently certified FSC paper
to ensure responsible forest management

For more information visit: www.harpercollins.co.uk/green

For my mother, Michele

And in loving memory of Maggie Estep

Girls are cruelest to themselves.

Anne Carson, *The Glass Essay*

What I know for certain about this time: My pupils were expanding. I never figured out if this was a symptom of falling in love or a side effect of the Chinese herbs my transgender friend Nathan was hooking me up with. Either way, I was stoked because I read an article that explained you are perceived as prettier when your pupils are dilated. A few years later, my pupils have shrunk back to their regular size, staring back at me, sometimes small as pinheads, each morning. But I don't take the Chinese herbs anymore either, so, who can really know.

Sometimes I wonder what it is I could tell you about her for my job here to be done. I am looking for a shortcut – something I could say that would effortlessly untangle the ball of yarn I am trying to untangle here on these pages. But that would be asking too much from you. It wasn't you who loved her, or thought you loved her. I wonder what I could write that would help you to understand that it is profoundly easy to fall in love with an olive-skinned woman that touches you *just so*, and who has a tattoo of a quote from *Orlando* trailing down her back. *Show me your tattoo again*, I'd say in bed. She'd pull up the bottom of her shirt, and I'd trace my fingers over the cursive words by

Virginia Woolf that read: *Love, the poet said, is a woman's whole existence.*

My mother still lives in the house in which I was raised – a woodland cottage in a small hamlet in the country. As a child, I adored the woods and spent the days playing in streams, sitting on my singing rock making up songs, crowning my head with dandelions and using berries as lipstick. I loved chewing on mint leaves and chives. My mom showed me how to soak Queen Anne's lace in food coloring overnight and we'd wake in the morning to bright pink and blue flowers. We often took walks in the woods, sometimes together, sometimes alone. In my teenage years, it was inevitable that after an argument, the door would slam and one of us would trudge off toward the woods. When I was sixteen, a lesbian couple in their forties built a house across the woods from us. This was significant as we'd never had any neighbors. The woods behind the house were chaotic. Walking through you were bound to return home with scratches and tick bites. But when the lesbians moved in, they landscaped the woods so that there would be a loop on which they were able to walk their dogs. Right away, my mom took to walking the circle as well. We'd leave notes for each other on the kitchen counter, *Went to walk the circle.* The lesbians were an intriguing couple, one was wealthy and of some notoriety, the other a struggling artist. My mom often chided me when I was a teenager for calling them 'the lesbians' but the only reason I called them that was because she did.

Ten years later, in late summer, some nights before I move out of my mother's house, she takes a gig dog sitting the lesbians' poodles, and I join her. We pack overnight bags and cut through the woods to their home. Their house is something out of *Home & Gardening* magazine. There have been articles written about the house describing how it is 'non-toxic' and 'cutting-edge.' While the sun goes down, we sit outside, marveling at the view, drinking expensive wine from their wine cellar and eating their exotic cheeses. While we have a warm buzz, we get the idea to pull the pillows off of the lounge chairs, lug them up the hill. We lie on our backs, giggling, looking at the stars, pointing out constellations. I remember thinking to myself that this was one of the best nights I'd ever spent with my mother. I felt content in her company, like there was no one else I'd rather be with. As though I never wanted to leave. But a few days later, I left. I boarded a plane and was gone.

Your book was amazing. These were the first words Finn said to me. She wrote them on my Facebook wall when I still lived with my mother. I'd been visiting Finn's city frequently, to see friends and attend literary events, but Finn and I had not yet met in person. We began emailing, discussing books and authors we loved and didn't. I enjoyed our back and forth; she was witty and verbose. There was talk of meeting for coffee together on my next visit. I would be in town to do a reading that summer. My mother was coming with me – we were making a mini-vacation out of it.

We never did get coffee that summer, but Finn attended my reading. I took a photograph of her. We'd barely talked thirty seconds and looking back I find it odd I would take a picture of someone I did not know, while they were not looking. I carry the image of her from that day in my mind. Cocky smirk of a smile. Slouched posture. Men's jeans that looked both broken-in and new. A long-sleeved shirt, soft, semi-fitted. A baseball hat. Arms crossed against her chest. Sneakers. Leaning her weight back onto one foot. She'd come alone to the reading. The sun is hitting her face and the grass she's standing on is bright green. In the photograph, I can see half of my mother's body – she's standing just a foot away from Finn, though they never met. I do not remember who introduced Finn and me, if we were introduced. I do not remember what Finn said to me and I do not remember what I said to her. I do remember I was flirtatiously calling her by both her first and last name. I'd been drinking wine with my mom before the reading, and continued to drink at the park to calm my nerves. When the reading ended, I watched her saunter off. The weather was impeccable, I was drunk, and she somewhat intrigued me. The next morning, Finn emailed to say that she had loved my reading; that I should do more readings. I do not know where this photograph is though I have spent time searching for it. By the time this book is published, the photograph will be three years old.

Three months after I took the photograph, I moved to the city Finn lived in for various reasons, none of them Finn. I needed a change – I was becoming a bit too comfortable living at home, and pain pills were becoming a casual part of my life, too easy to find in my small town. I was snorting opiates a few times a week and hating myself for it. Moving to a new city meant an absence of drug connections. I'd also met a guy named Isaac through a mutual friend, and we'd begun dating long-distance. I knew I wouldn't be with Isaac forever as we didn't have a passionate connection. We were quite different. For one, he didn't do opiates, he was more interested in sports than books, but he was kind and smart – and I wanted to surround myself with drug-free people. We enjoyed each other, and the relationship was benign, and I thought it would be good for me. He offered for me to stay with him until I found a place of my own, and I took him up on it.

On a Sunday morning after the move I was messaging with Finn on Facebook while Isaac was watching football and we were drinking coffee. Finn said she was watching football and drinking coffee too. *Finn's really cool, don't you think?* I said to Isaac, who had met her at the same reading. He agreed, *I don't know her well, but she does seem pretty cool.*

Isaac and I broke it off about a month after this exchange (the break-up consisting of two low-drama text messages – me saying, *I think we're better off as friends*, and him replying, *Yeah, you're probably right*). This cleared a place for Finn, and she slowly began to fill up my life.

I don't know if I will be able to get you to see her the way I saw her. I worry that if I cannot make you fall in love with her inexplicably, inexorably, and immediately, the way I did, then you will not be experiencing this book in the way I hope you will. When my editor read the original manuscript, she sent me a text message that said, *I'm falling in love with Finn from the details in the opening paragraphs.*

But it is now occurring to me that by offering you these details about Finn, I could ruin things for you as well. I could tell you her favorite book of poetry or how she liked her hamburgers cooked, or the words tattooed across her knuckles. But depending on what I tell you, I could lose you. So I'll tell you some things, leave out others.

I never knew her birth name. She would not reveal this. She'd changed it to Finn when she was twenty-two, long before I met her. She liked drinking Salty Dogs and champagne and dark beers. She was nineteen years older than I was and called me 'champ.' She wore men's clothes, usually from high-end shops and she wore her jeans slung low. She had friendly-looking crow's feet around her eyes when she laughed. Her eyes changed from blue-green to gray, and when she was happy, they looked almost yellow. She had hairless skin like velvet. I feel like people say this a lot and it should be banned from all books, but she smelled like cocoa butter. She read books avidly. She walked with a certain swagger. My friend Nathan saw her walking down the street, and told me, *I can't tell if she's incredibly cocky or incredibly tortured.*

It would be unfair for me to keep this from you: Finn was gay and in a long-term relationship with a woman. They lived together. They had for ten years.

Isn't it sad to talk about ex-lovers in the past tense as though they are dead? I have a friend who this immensely bothers. He claims he wants to fill a red wagon with the women he's loved, but he doesn't want to let go of one woman to put in another.

The first few months after my move, I am unemployed. I live on bagels and energy bars, soup and ramen noodles. I apply for food stamps, which I qualify for, but I miss one of the questions and am too lazy to re-apply. During this time, Finn emails me and says that she knows it is hard to be new in a city. She says if I need a laugh, she'll meet me for a beer. The first time we meet alone for a drink, she shows up with a collection of short stories in her hand, and tells me I can keep it. It is fall, and we sit outside at a picnic table, across from one another. Growing increasingly drunk over IPAs, I pull out a piece of paper. We exchange stories, adventures we've had, and tales of heartbreak. *You have to write about that!* we say. We scrawl down lists of titles for each other to write stories about. I remember waking up and finding the list in my wallet. I held onto it for months, until finally I misplaced it, or it was thrown out. It's probably in a book somewhere.

Finn and I usually hug when we part ways. I feel comfortable around her and she seems to see me in a good light – as if I can do no wrong. I show her stories I am writing and she is unconditionally supportive. She champions me, saying things like *I got you.* If I put myself down, she counters it. *I talk too much*, I say once. *You do not talk too much. Talk more*, she answers. She tells me I am special, that I am golden. She is effusive in her emails, effusive in person. I feel if I need something like five dollars or a ride somewhere, she will give me those things. This feels important, as I am new to the city, do not have many friends yet, and do not have a support system.

Around Thanksgiving, I apply for a job at the Public Library. Finn has worked at this library, and encourages me to do so. I am hired for an entry-level position. My title is 'Library Page.' I am responsible for placing the returned books back on the shelves, and some days I have to shelf-read to make sure the books are in order according to the Dewey Decimal System. I like the job, despite its obvious monotony, as it allows me to live in my head. I love peeking through the aisles of books and spying on people. I fantasize that I will lock eyes with someone, and they will turn out to be my soul mate. My co-workers range from bored college students to elderly women who have been working at the library for twenty years. Finn would be working at the same library, but she's recently been promoted to another branch, as a technical service librarian. On foot, the libraries are thirty minutes apart.

I know I find Finn's aesthetic attractive, but I haven't yet explored feelings of being attracted to her, in part because I haven't yet explored my ability to fall for a woman. I figure if I was going to be with a woman, I would have been with one by now. I would know if I was bisexual or gay. Being a writer, I assume I am at least mildly self-aware. It also has not occurred to me that Finn might be attracted to me. It doesn't occur to me she might be interested in me as more than a friend.

It doesn't occur to me, even though she writes me an email in which she says she wants me to read on a barstool under dim lights for her while she sips on a beer. *Yeah, book it,* her email ends. *Book it.* And I do vaguely remember staring at her brown hands while she spoke, her knuckle tattoos, thinking they were the most beautiful hands I'd ever seen.

It is the night before New Year's Eve. Finn has just returned from visiting her family in Florida for the holidays and when she got back, her girlfriend left to visit her own. This leaves Finn and me alone in the city with no plans for the weekend. After some Facebook messaging, she drives over to where I am house sitting. I have changed into a blue and white baseball shirt and gold hoop earrings. I don't know what to wear, and want to look tomboyish, not super girly. I don't know what Finn likes. And, apparently, I care.

When she arrives, the energy between us is palpable. I offer her a drink and we both sort of pace around each other, making observations about the apartment. She sees the self-help book *Women's Moods* on my bed, picks it up, studies the cover and before chucking it back down, jokes, *I know everything in here, whatchu wanna know?* (It would turn out she actually didn't know everything in there. Neither of us knew how volatile my moods would become.)

We finish our beers, leave the apartment and walk to the bar. It is a cold night. I wear an enormous winter coat, Finn has on only a hooded sweatshirt. At the bar she orders a beer sample platter for us to share. I say, *I never go out and drink with anyone anymore*, and she says, *Neither do I!* She reaches across the table and begins going through my wallet. She sees tons of unnecessary business cards and says, *Jeez, dude.* She takes out a New York Public Library card I have, and says, *This is the coolest thing you have.* Emboldened by the beers, after an hour or so, I tell Finn that I don't understand how lesbians have sex. *Dildo?* I ask. *Vibrator? Fingering? Humping?* She shrugs, clearly amused. *It's different for everyone*, she says. *It's different every time.*

Finn gets a rise out of engaging with strangers and I love watching her do it. People sometimes approach her when we're out, telling her she looks like someone they know. She is charming and can hold conversations. We meet a guy with weed cookies and convince him to give us a couple, which we quickly eat. We meet a guy who stutters. (*Who meets a stutterer?* we ask ourselves, laughing for weeks after.) Like in that book about animals, *Unlikely Friendships*, we are an unlikely pair, and when the stutterer asks us how we know each other, one of us says, *We're cousins*, and he believes us. When we return to my apartment, we sit on the couch and roll a joint with a page from a book since we don't have rolling papers. Finn walks around the room commenting on the books on the shelves. She is hard on books, making snobby, but humorous, comments. We lie in bed together, stoned from the cookies. The bed is against a brick wall and I begin to imagine we are alone in a different city together. *Let's pretend we're in Paris or Brooklyn*, I say.

Finn gives me her sweatshirt to wear that night. I fall asleep in it. Later, she wakes me to retrieve it, smoothing her hand over my temples, kissing my forehead, before leaving.

The next night, New Year's Eve, she emails and asks what I'm doing. *I probably won't want to do something but will*, she says. *I'm the opposite, probably will want to do something but won't*, I reply. I've been invited to a party of an acquaintance, so I ask Finn if she wants to go with me. She says yes, and picks me up. I went to the hair salon that day and paid too much money for highlights. My hair is blonder than usual. *The hair is good*, Finn says to me, flashing her white teeth, *It'll turn heads*. The party is low-key, almost boring, and Finn and I plant ourselves in the living room, mainly socializing with each other. I am sitting across from Finn on the couch, and she is in a chair. She pats her lap and points to my feet. I move them into her lap, as though this is the most natural thing for me to do, and Finn works them with her hands nonchalantly, as though this is nothing new either. Later, a guy at the party mistakes us for a couple. Neither of us minds, we laugh, possibly it's what we were after.

After midnight Finn asks do I want a ride home or do I want to sleep over and I say, sleep over. When we get to her bedroom, she asks do I want shorts or pants to sleep in, and I say, pants. She lends me a T-shirt that says *I Don't Do Drugs I Am Drugs*, on it. I am on the inside of the bed near the window. Finn is standing near the dresser and she says, *You're in my bed!* She sounds bewildered, triumphant, amused. (She would speak with this exact intonation two more times, when we weren't just friends anymore, when we were beginning to fuck, to fall in love: *You answered the door in a towel!* and *You sat on my lap!*) And though we're just friends, she puts her arms around me, asking, *Is this okay?* I tell her it's okay. We say goodnight. *I can't sleep*, I say, a few moments later. *I know, me either*, she laughs, *tell me a story*. I cannot think of anything interesting, and I mumble and slur in a drunken stupor until I fall asleep.

We wake in the same position we fell asleep in. I move the curtain from the window to check the weather. The sun surprises me. *Sun! The sun is out!* I start saying that sort of thing. Finn stands in the doorway, watching me. *I think it's cute when people are excited about the sun*, she says. Instead of going to change in the bathroom, I change out of her shirt and back into my dress while still in her bed. I feel self-conscious though, and aware of it, wondering if it is too intimate an act. While Finn is in the bathroom, I look around the apartment. Everything is in its right place. Knick-knacks and what look like expensive Japanese paintings on the walls. I wonder which one of them – Finn or her girlfriend – is the lover of Japanese art. I see no photos of her girlfriend, though I try not to look. I let my eyes be lazy. As we walk out of her apartment building, Finn mentions that she isn't going to tell her girlfriend that I slept over, because she wouldn't understand. *Okay. Right*, I say. Besides, nothing happened. What is there to tell? I understand and yet I don't understand.

While Finn drives us downtown, we sing along with the radio. She tells me it's the first time in a decade she hasn't taken a shower before work and I say something like, *Man, you gotta loosen up*. She smiles. In this moment I remember noticing myself affecting her habits, in what could be considered either a negative or positive way. We park and decide we want to grab coffees to bring to work. It is one of those days that feels fake or cinematic, because parking is free and the streets are dead. I feel like I'm on a movie set. My mom calls my cell phone. I answer, telling her I'm with Finn. Finn and I are both smiling and laughing. (Later Finn told me I looked beautiful that day, with sun on my newly lightened hair. She said my eyes lit up when my mom called.) We order our coffees and Finn insists on buying mine. We hug before we go our separate ways. A couple weeks later Finn emails me a song, says it reminds her a little of us. The lyrics are about waking up hungover with someone, about watching them get dressed as you block the sun from your face.

I excitedly tell one of my bisexual friends about my weekend. She shakes her head. *You guys shouldn't do that.* I play dumb and ask, *Why not?* She raises her voice and says, *Because you're not a lesbian! Because she has a girlfriend!*

She is hot, though, she adds, and I agree.

When my father visits, I show him the city on foot, walk to restaurants, and take him to plays. It is good to see my father, who I consider one of my closest friends, and I enjoy showing him what my life is like in this city. I invite Finn to meet us for coffee. She will be the only friend he meets. My dad and I arrive at the café first. Finn walks in a few minutes later, and immediately I can tell she is not what he is expecting. She tells him her name. He flinches, and I wonder if Finn notices this too. He wants to know what Finn is short for. *Nothing*, she says, winking at me. She walks to the counter and orders a coffee. The three of us talk about writing, a reading Finn recently attended, what plans my dad and I have for the rest of his visit. Finn hugs me before she returns to work. Her sweatshirt is white, pristine. After I hug her, I notice some of my makeup has rubbed off on her shoulder. I feel humiliated and pray she doesn't see it. Finn is fastidious in her appearance, everything always looks brand new, clean.

My dad reiterates twice how much he enjoyed Finn. *I liked her a lot*, he says. *She's really sharp.* Looking back, I find it odd I invited her to meet my father. I had other friends I could have invited, yet I chose her. By this time I had made some girl friends, co-workers who were closer to me in age, but it was not important to me that he meet them, only that he meet Finn.

On an unusually warm winter Friday, so warm I am wearing a tank top, Finn comes over for drinks and to see my new place. I am renting a renovated basement from our mutual friend Shannon, who works with me at the library. I have a photograph a friend took of me in the park just hours before Finn came over. I am jumping. Wearing jeans and a tank top. In the bright sun, on the green grass. I'd been drinking coffee into the evening, and it made me feel frisky. Before Finn comes over, I take a shower, put my hair up. When she arrives, the three of us sit in the living room and drink whiskey and Cokes. After a while, Finn gets up from the chair she's in and sits on my legs, which are stretched out the length of the couch. We are talking, making flirtatious banter. I'm complaining about my male co-workers and Finn shakes her head and says, *See, I don't hate men, I just think they're stupid.*

While Finn is sitting on my legs, Shannon, who is smoking a cigarette across from us, furrows her forehead, rolls her eyeballs, and says, *Go have sex.* Even in that moment, I don't think we will have sex. Ha-ha funny, hysterical. Having sex doesn't occur to me. How does one have sex with a woman? Besides, I'm straight. But I do take Finn's hand. I am sitting up now, next to her, Indian-style, and under the blanket I take her soft hand in mine, then rest it on my thigh. We quietly sit that way for the rest of the night, never letting go of each other's hands. After midnight, when I announce I am going to bed, Finn follows me downstairs to the basement to say goodnight. The walls are teal and we will take to calling my basement apartment The Aquarium. Finn first goes to the bathroom, and when she gets downstairs, I am already in my pajamas, in bed. She lies next to me and I turn toward her and we are kissing. Completely unspoken – there is no conversation such as: *Can I kiss you?* or *Is this okay?* As she describes it later, there is no teeth clanking, no awkwardness, just fucking, and no fumbling. In my head I think something like: *So this is how they do it.* Her hand up my T-shirt, her palm tenderly placed on my lower back. Her mouth open and warm.

In my memory it happens quickly – everything of hers in everything of mine. Fingers and tongue. Her palms on my back, her hands in my hair, her breath in my ear saying *babybabybaby. I want you so bad*, I say. I remember this surprising me. It rolled out of my mouth so naturally: *I want you so bad.* Where did it come from? Since when had I wanted her so bad? Why had I not been conscious of it? She puts me in different positions: fucks me from behind with her hand, on her face, against the wall, on the bedroom carpet. I moan. At one point I ask her how many and what is inside of me, and she laughs and says she doesn't even know. *Go have sex.*

Never have I ever had sex with a woman. I don't want to take my leggings off because my legs aren't shaved. It is winter and I haven't been having sex so I haven't shaved in weeks and now I am embarrassed. But Finn says, *Girls don't care about things like that.* At the edge of the bed, after we both finish, she smooths my hair from my forehead and says, *I could totally fall in love with you. How do you know I'm already not?* I begin to cry. I am already aware this will not turn out well. We are both aware. When I start crying, she says, *Oh no, what are we doing – this is not what you need.* No, it was not what I needed. But maybe what I wanted.

Waking up the next morning, I feel as though I am a different person. I feel high, invigorated with adrenaline. I call my best friend, Lily, and tell her what happened. *Was it like, the best head of your life?* she asks. I have an email from Finn, checking to make sure I am okay. I write back, telling her I'm great. Better than ever. And she says, *Who fucking knew, right? It's like we starred in our own movie last night.* She calls me after we email. When I answer the phone, we both immediately begin laughing. We keep laughing and laughing together. From nerves and from how ridiculous our night seemed.

Finn tells me on her drive home she saw a cop. *If they pulled me over I would have been screwed*, she says, *because I smelled like whiskey, wine, and pussy.* We decide we want to hang out again tonight, and that Finn will meet me where I am babysitting.

The kids are asleep when Finn shows up and we sit on opposite ends of the couch watching *Seinfeld* on TV. We're shy about touching now, after all the fucking. She drives us back to The Aquarium where I take a shower after setting her up with an episode of *The Sopranos.* I love seeing her comfortable in my bed, hearing her laughter as I shower. I get into the bed with wet hair and we sleep some, kiss some, and talk some. We're both drained, emotionally, physically. She leaves in the wee hours of the morning to let out her dog.

Sunday night I call her to come back *again*. I am upstairs drinking wine with my roommate but I lie and say I have to go to the basement and Skype with my mom because my roommate knows Finn has a girlfriend. Finn drives back over and sneaks through the back door. We've been in bed making love for three days and no one but us knows. She tells me about the song 'Those Three Days' by Lucinda Williams. Later I will learn how terrified she is of anything dark or depressing – films or music or literature, so looking back, I am surprised she suggested we listen to that song. She did warn me ahead of time, *Maybe we shouldn't, it's depressing.* But I want to, and she holds me while we listen to it, not talking. In the early morning, when she is getting ready to leave, she stands at the foot of my bed. She finds my foot under the comforter and lifts it to her lips, kisses it, sets it back down. *I don't know any other way to say this, but you rock my world*, she says. We both giggle. Well, she chuckles. (*Girls like me don't giggle*, she says.)

A few hours later my phone interrupts my sleep. It's Finn. She says she wanted to hear my voice. She has left work for her lunch break and is walking to buy a slice of pizza. She tells me she is trying to write about our past three days, but all she comes up with is *blue and womb and holy fucking hell.* Our conversation goes:

F: *Sometimes on* American Idol*, Nicki Minaj says, I'm obsessed with you.*

Me: *I'm obsessed with you right now.*

F: *I'm so obsessed with you right now.*

We laugh. She does end up writing about our time in The Aquarium. She reads me a poem she wrote about us. The poem says she knew the *we* or *us* of *this* would never make it out of that ocean-colored room but that she loved me anyway. The poem says, *You were already in your pajamas, but I fucked you anyway, because sometimes life writes itself.*

Things seem to accelerate overnight. We are all over each other with sweet words. We send each other sentences: Maggie Nelson and Rebecca Solnit and Mary Ruefle and Katherine Angel and Susan Minot and Adrienne Rich and Alejandro Zambra and Ivan Coyote. We text or email photos of sentences. I no longer remember the origin of most of them. They are pasted un-referenced into a document on my computer:

What I know: When I met you, a blue rush began.

We treat desire as a problem to be solved.

We fucked for six straight hours that afternoon, which does not seem precisely possible but that is what the clock said. We killed the time.

To read is to cover one's face, to write is to show it.

Are there many things in this cool-hearted world so utterly exquisite as the pure love of one woman for another woman?

Finn tells me she sits and stares at her email account as though she is about to win the lottery. She sends me a song called 'Vagitarian (Lesbian Love Song)' that won't work but I keep the file downloaded onto my computer for months anyway, until I eventually move it into the recycle bin. She knows my hours at the library and often times her emails to my schedule. She is a night emailer; I email in the mornings. She has insomnia; I sleep like a baby. When I leave work at nine p.m., there are emails and texts from her waiting to be read. The bus drops me off in my neighborhood and nothing but 7-Eleven is open. I buy red boxed wine and a Hershey bar and walk home to sit in bed and email with Finn until we fall asleep and wake up to start doing it again.

Just before I came to this city, my mother told me life could be exciting without drugs. After having sex with Finn, I begin to agree with my mother. I've never had a therapist before but in this city everyone seems to have both a therapist and an acupuncturist. After a weekend of avoidant behavior, spent eating my weight in macaroni and cheese while watching *Mermaids*, I decide, hey, maybe I could use someone to talk to. I Google therapists and 'Borderline Personality Disorder' because after reading about Borderline Personality Disorder – 'tendency to act impulsively without considering consequences' – I believe I might qualify. I find a woman named Karma and I call her but she is a hundred dollars per session and I quickly hang up. I find a woman with long red hair. She is smiling in her online photo, her arm around a dog. I call her. Her voice is meek, but she sounds nurturing, like I can trust her.

Dr. Kay's office is on the third floor of a large building. The room is spacious with two windows. Through them there is a large tree I grow accustomed to staring at through each season. The walls are the same color paint as The Aquarium. The furniture is Ikea-style. Dr. Kay wears cardigans and flats. She never takes notes while I talk but she remembers everything. My instinct in life is to avoid commitments, but I never miss a week of therapy. I love having this woman's full attention, I love the way she looks at me while I talk, I love the way her eyes tear up when mine do.

Does your therapist think I'm bad for you? Finn asks. *I don't want to be bad for you.*

As a writer it is inspiring to work at a library, to see so many people reading and borrowing books, writing in notebooks and on computers. I feel validated. The library carries my first book and sometimes girls approach me at the counter, recognizing me from my author photo. I sometimes complain about this to friends and co-workers but secretly I love when this happens.

My shifts are short, just three hours, sometimes four. Sunday afternoons are my favorite because I work with Nathan. We eat chocolate bars, drink coffee and listen to the CDs that get checked in during our shift while we close up. Nathan drives me home most evenings, and we often stop at Wendy's to get 99-cent chicken nuggets and fries.

Finn gives me a choice: do I want to wear her flannel shirt or her sweatshirt or her leather jacket. It's a few weeks after the first time we slept together, and it's a week night. I choose the flannel because I've already worn the sweatshirt and jacket and I like to wear as many different pieces of clothing of other people's as I can. Finn fingers me under the table, under my dress, which makes this easier. When Finn and I are drinking in dark bars, we forget we are in public, it's as though we go underwater. When we finish kissing, she pulls away and looks around, saying, *Woah, everything is still here.* We spend the nights looking at each other and not much else. Unlike other times – cafés in daylight – when she is careful about touching my hands, aware someone from the library might walk by.

Come home with me, she says three times in my ear. She is too drunk to steer her bike home, she thinks she is going to puke, she thinks I roofied her drink, so I walk her bike and she stumbles along next to me. This is the first time she has drunk more than I have. We fall asleep holding each other and wake up early, finding each other's bodies and mouths. She traces my stomach and hip bones and underwear. *What are these underwear? What do they look like?* She keeps touching me as I tell her they are gray, and some kind of lace, and cheap. She says, *They feel so rough like they will never come off, like even if there was a war they would still stay on.* Then she says gray is her favorite color.

When we wake for a second time later in the morning, she says, half joking, *How'd you get in my bed?* I tell her, *You asked me to come. Three times.* She has a stomachache. We discuss that it is probably psychosomatic. She is down, depressed, saying she feels bouts of guilt and shame. She doesn't have to say it out loud, I know it is because of her girlfriend. She calls in late to work. We stay in bed, touching, being sweet, and being sad. *You're like a soft little animal,* I say, while we're nuzzling each other. Her voice so small and amused when she repeats back: *I'm like a soft little animal?*

She even keeps her sneakers on while she fucks me, sometimes. My clothes off, hers on. *How did you know not to touch her? It's like you had a sixth sense,* a friend says. It's not that I had a sixth sense, it was so apparent to me. We were involved in a power play. *Everything you do is what I want you to do,* I said once, and before I was done with my sentence she was beginning hers, *Everything you do is exactly what I want you to do!* At the bar, before she fingered me, she was sitting on the inside and I was on the outside. She asked me to switch places with her. And then when I didn't do it, she insisted. I bring this up in the morning: *You made me switch spots with you last night*, I say. *But wasn't it better that way?* she asks. *It was the same*, I reply.

Lesbians can suck my dick! They will ruin your life. I tell the bartender this after my second tequila shot. He responds by asking if I'd like a glass of water. It's a Friday night and Finn won't meet me at the bar near her apartment where I am taking tequila shots, so I break my phone. I know she is able to meet me – that her girlfriend is out of town and that this is a choice she is (or is not) making. I am livid and I throw my phone as hard as I can twice against a brick wall and then chuck it into the street and watch a car run it over. I do this mid phone call to Finn so she can hear how angry I am. I am a child. I have regressed several years emotionally. When I fetch the phone from the middle of the street Finn is still on the line. She tells me to stay where I am, that she will come pick me up. I sit on the pavement to wait, numb now from the tequila. When she pulls up in her Jeep, she says: *You are in so much trouble right now.* I find this funny. I like seeing her anger. Her anger does not scare me. I am provoking it. She drives me home and we sit in her car parked outside The Aquarium until three in the morning, arguing. I scream at her that she is no better than a man. She engages a bit. She yells, *I never said I was going to leave my relationship!* Immediately I feel sick.

I slam the Jeep door. She yells at me to grow up, throws my jacket out of the car. Miraculously, my phone continues to work but I can only read the text messages two words at a time. I tell her about this and she texts me in the morning, writing:

Are you
Okay

I respond:

I am
Awesome

She says:

Yeah you
Are

The quick transitions between bliss and hell, between our fights and apologies, are so extreme, so jolting. It feels so different from the men I have dated, who refused to engage in this sort of drama. Finn seems to be able to stomach it. In retrospect, I think I may have been testing her, pushing her, trying to scare her away. Not knowing how to walk away on my own.

The morning after the phone and tequila episode, I expect Finn to be done with me. Instead, she writes me an email telling me it is okay – *yes, it was a crazy night – but that is to be expected, it has been a crazy month.* After I have behaved so poorly, so ridiculously, she compliments me. She tells me I have an amazing mind. She tells me she watches my mind twist and turn and figure things out. She tells me on Sunday we can hang out all day. We'll spend the day together, have coffee. She promises. I'm still in bed. I still feel the tequila, and I call my mom. I tell her about Finn. I tell her I think I'm a lesbian. More correctly, I tell her, *I wanna be a lesbian.* She sounds concerned. My voice is small, exhausted. She mishears. *You don't wanna be or you want to be?* she asks. A few weeks later I receive a letter in the mail from my mom. She is concerned but supportive. She will support me either way. I ask Finn if things are always this insane and dramatic between two women, and she says yes. She says it's either like this, or monotonous and boring. As if there is no in-between.

Sunday morning I wake naturally with the sun. Finn drives to my neighborhood and parks at a coffee shop. I walk from my apartment toward the coffee shop and she walks toward me so we will meet halfway. I carry a daffodil with me. When we meet each other, we turn around and go back toward the café. She goes to the counter and buys us mugs of coffee. She gets us glasses of water. She eats a muffin and I point out that she did not offer me a piece. I write in my journal and she writes on her computer. She uses the restroom and when she returns, she stands behind me and puts her hands on my shoulders, squeezes. I recoil. I explain it is difficult for me to be touched if we aren't going to have sex. After what happened last night, we have both agreed we cannot have sex. She apologizes. She says she wants me to know she still feels the same, that she still loves me, even after my episode. When we leave the café it is early evening. We walk to Finn's car, which is parked outside of a lesbian bar. There's a group of women outside, drinking and smoking. Finn and I get into her car and she says, *All those dykes were looking at you. They were jealous you were getting in the car with me.* Nah, I say. *You're sexy, don't you know that?* she says. *No, you are*, I say.

She drives me home. I am grateful she has spent the day with me – that she is giving me attention and affection. *Will you kiss me at least?* I say, and she nods, though we both keep staring forward. She turns to me, grabs at the back of my head. The kiss is long and passionate. When we break apart, she says, *How do we do that? I've never kissed anyone like that in my life.* We both face the windshield. Down the street is a house with a bright blue door. *Is that door the same color as The Aquarium?* she asks. *Almost, wanna come see?* I say. She nods and says, *Yeah, for a minute. Or maybe a few minutes.*

I try to conceal my astonishment. Finn follows me down the stairs. My room is messy. I flop onto my bed, I am showing her a story I've published in a literary magazine. She lies next to me on the bed, reads over my shoulder. We are both chewing gum. We throw it out of our mouths onto my dresser. She is excited because her gum landed on the inside of a bracelet on the dresser. *Look! Look where my gum landed!* The day before, she has gotten a new tattoo, an image of Harriet the Spy on her shoulder. While we make out, she reminds me, *Hey, watch my shoulder, watch my shoulder.*

I tell Finn I'm worried her rings are going to come off inside me. I am terrified of things getting stuck inside my vagina, though nothing like that has ever happened. Whenever we have sex, Finn throws one of her back ribs out and can feel it for weeks afterward. My right shoulder blade is always bothering me. I'm hyper-aware of it sticking out of my back. She calls it my wing. I love asking her, *Will you fix my wing?* When I ask that, she nods, turns me onto my back and touches my shoulder blade tenderly. She takes my hand, stretches my arm out, and moves it in circles, coaxes it back into place. Tonight while she's doing this it is quiet until she says, *I don't know, when you moved here, I felt like you belonged to me.* I feel cared for in this moment. I will cling to this memory for the next few months, as I feel less and less cared for by Finn.

She unbuttons my shirt. Underneath I am wearing a lace tank top. *What is this shirt?* she says. *This shirt is going to haunt me.* We kiss and kiss and then she turns me around, fucking me from behind with her hand, pulling my underwear to the side. I keep my tank top on. *I like fucking you while you still have some clothes on*, she says. We laugh after I come. *Let's make you come again, because it's fun*, she says. I ask her if she came and she says, *Did it feel like I came?* I ask her if she wants to see the new lingerie I bought. She says yes. I leave the bed and walk to my dresser, opening the top drawer, stripping my clothes off and pulling the pink and lacey dress over my head. She lies on her back on the carpet and I lie on top of her.

She says, *If you fall in love with someone else, will you tell me?* I ask her why. *So I can be happy for you, and sad for me*, she says, and we both laugh a little. Then she mumbles, *I don't want you to fall in love with anyone else.*

I always want to feel good and I never want to feel bad. Because of this, I'm experienced in substance abuse issues. When something feels good or tastes good it's a struggle for me to use moderation. I never want to feel okay – I want to feel better than average. This is something I realize I cannot sustain. Sex with Finn feels good, is unsustainable, because she is in a relationship. It's another narcotic of sorts. Oxytocin and OxyContin are a close comparison. It is not lost on me that Finn shares a name with my ex-drug dealer. It's a coincidence, sure, and it is oversimplifying to say that when I shook my drug addiction, I placed my addictive behaviors on Finn. But it also would not be fair if I left it out. With Finn, I have found a new drug. A reason to wake up in the morning. She is my source of feeling confident in the world; with Finn I feel attractive, smart, loved, the same way I'd feel if I were putting opiates up my nose.

Like church, my therapy sessions are on Sunday mornings. In the room with the blue walls I explore terms I have previously not given much thought. *Boundaries. Emotional regulating. Verbal abuse. Emotional abuse. Gaslighting. Manipulation.* I tell Dr. Kay I don't know if I've ever learned to *deal* with my emotions. *Well, have you?* she asks me. I buy a workbook after our session called *Don't Let Your Emotions Run Your Life.* Ever since I quit using drugs, I am terrified of my feelings. I know drugs aren't an option for me, but I am scared of depression, so au naturel uppers are a new interest of mine. I pop tons of vitamins. I buy St. John's wort and vitamin D and 5-HTP. I bring them everywhere with me. I pull them out and swallow them at bars with my beers. Even vitamins I cannot use responsibly. I take them in public, happy to pop something that is socially acceptable. I go to therapy weekly. I take my Chinese herbs in both liquid and capsule form.

It surprises me, given my liberal upbringing, to realize how undereducated in gender studies and gay rights I am. My mother passionately enforced equality, talked about race, bought me black baby dolls instead of white ones. But I don't have many memories of talking about homosexuality with her. In middle school and high school I experimented a bit – drunk at parties, my best friends and I would kiss with tongues. But it seemed like something we were doing to impress our boyfriends – a kind of look-how-I'll-do-anything mentality. In my early twenties I'd been all over the map. I'd lived in New York City and Europe and experimented widely with sex and drugs, but even then, aside from going to a gay bar once, and having a gay male co-worker, I wasn't close with any gay people. I didn't notice if people were gay. I didn't care. I didn't think about it much. In high school you could count the number of overtly gay kids on one hand. So it wasn't until I met Finn that I found myself floundering, questioning my sexuality, grasping for an answer. In therapy, I was noticing my tendency to view things in such black and white colors. And here it was coming up again, with regard to my sexuality. I did not know if I was gay or straight. This or that. Being in the middle was somewhere I did not know how to be. Finn and I talked about this. I'd often state that writer's block did not exist. *Like bisexuality*, she'd say. *Just kidding, bisexuals are probably just early signs of evolution.*

On a park bench one evening, after Finn gets out of work, and before I go in, I read her poems from *A Dream of a Common Language.* She says Adrienne Rich scares her a little. I am learning that many things scare her a little. She has a Tea Tree toothpick in her mouth. She has the posture of a teenaged boy. I want to pummel her, wrestle her in the grass, give her new blue jeans grass stains, hump her leg. *When was the last time someone read you poems in a park?* I ask her. *Never*, she says, smiling. I feel like I'm doing most of the talking so I ask her if there's anything she wants to tell me. *Yeah*, she says. *When we were little, living in Florida, we called rooms in our house the blue room and the green room. Even though the walls aren't green anymore, I still ask if I'm sleeping in the green room.*

When she hugs me, she speaks into my ear, tells me she loves me. She is always smaller in reality than she is in my head. Smaller shoulders, shorter. When I tell her this, she tells me that is strange, because when she catches glimpses of herself in the mirror or storefront windows, she also is smaller than she imagines. We walk together to the street corner. A homeless man on the bench has been muttering at us while we sat, and while Finn and I walk away, I turn at him and say, *See ya.* Finn looks at me, perplexed, and says, *That was so cute how you said 'see ya' to him.*

We fantasize sometimes. When Finn holds me, her legs tangled over mine, I mumble to her that if we dated, we would probably have a lot of problems, and she cracks up. *We would have so much make-up sex*, she says. *Who would cook?* we wonder. *Would our kids go to public school?* We fantasize about going to a dinner party together. Secretly I fantasize about more, always more. I imagine traveling Europe with Finn. I imagine sitting next to Finn on airplanes. I imagine road trips. I imagine her meeting my family. I imagine her coming with me to one of my readings, walking offstage to her. Nothing secret about it.

A few months earlier, when Finn and I were only friends, a girl named Sabine contacted me on Twitter to tell me that she sometimes read from my books on her webcam. One night I join the webcam and watch Sabine smoke weed and read from my book. She looks generally like a good time, with her short, pixie haircut and eyebrow ring. Sabine is a webcam girl and in a sex positive community in California, meaning she regularly practices polyamory. I do some research on her – read some interviews with her online. When my cell phone rings with an area code I don't recognize one morning, I answer it. It's Sabine, she's in town, and asks if I'd like to hang out. We meet in a café. She wears an enormous brass ring in the shape of a cowboy hat. She wears Doc Martens. She carries many bags and has a joint behind her ear. We walk to my apartment where she immediately begins to clean my room. I drink a glass of wine while she does this; I do not know what else to do. After, she tells me I am holding a great deal of tension in my chest, my pecs. She pulls different oils and lotions out of her backpack and sits me down on the bed. She says she will get the tightness out of my chest for me, and she gives me a brief massage. I don't know what to say while she does this, and I feel incredibly prudish in my pale pink cardigan buttoned up to the top. I can't remember the last time anyone gave me a massage.

After the massage, Sabine leaves to attend a reading. She leaves behind the brass cowgirl hat ring, which I take to wearing.

Finn notices the ring on my finger when we meet for coffee and I tell her all about Sabine. I am careful to mention that I am not attracted to Sabine in the same way I am attracted to her. *Well yeah, 'cause she's not in the sweet spot*, Finn says, matter-of-factly. *The sweet spot?* I ask. She explains to me she's spent decades trying to perfect the sweet spot. Butch, but soft. Right in between a male and female. I stare at her, listening. *Look at those little kid eyes!* she says and laughs.

Finn pretends sometimes that we are just friends. *We have to do things differently*, she says, *healthy*. So we try to be just friends. She asks me if I will meet her for a game of pinball, which turns into sex. When I ask her if she wants to come over and play Bananagrams, it turns into sex. We cannot be around each other without the strong desire to fuck.

Pizza is our food of choice. Food is an afterthought. We frequent four different pizza places during the months we see each other. When we go to bars near her house, we occasionally run into people she knows. We rarely run into people I know. She has a history here. She has a stable place to live and a job with benefits and security. She, with her thirties behind her, and me with mine yet to begin. Me with one suitcase, ready to leave at any time. Ready to jump in a car, buy a plane ticket. Goodbye. I haven't even opened a bank account in this city that I have lived in for almost a year. I like knowing I can flee. Au revoir, mon amie. Peace the hell out.

After sex with Finn, there is no clean-up time. There is no semen possibly inside of me. There are no bathroom trips. There is no worn-out towel laid down on the bed. No condoms on the floor or in the toilet. When we are done with sex we do not take separate bathroom trips. We stay in bed. Sleep, talk, fuck some more. There is so much kissing. There is deep delicious sleep. *That's my girl, sweet girl*, Finn tells me when she is making me come. Five months later, when she does not say these things anymore, I notice.

There are rug burns on my arms, Finn tells me. I ask why. *From holding you up*, she says, *from holding me up.*

My hands are my tools! Finn laughs.

Sabine visits me each season, so now she shows up along with the first signs of tulips and daffodils. When she arrives at The Aquarium, I say, *You look like Punky Brewster.* She's wearing a short denim skirt and her hair is long enough for a tiny ponytail. We both have on black boots and feather earrings. We eat MDMA and I get dressed in front of her. I ask her, *How do I look?* and she says, *You look like you wanna get fucked*, and we laugh. I think of Finn. I try to get my mind away from thoughts of her. This is easier around Sabine. It is only around Sabine that the anxiety of my situation with Finn lessens. With Sabine I am present, light, jubilant.

Sabine and I walk to a bar where a friend is reading. We sit in the front row, passing a plastic cup of wine back and forth. The MDMA is kicking in and I whisper, *You're like Jesus right now.* After the reading Sabine meets up with friends and I go to a restaurant and drink champagne with other friends, writers I know, none of whom seems to notice I am on MDMA.

In the morning Finn texts me *how are you* and I answer *I'm like really joyous and social* and she says *that's an amazing way to be.* Finn knows from Facebook photos that I am with Sabine. She has told me that Sabine bugs her. She has flippantly said she would like to punch Sabine in the face. But we both know she is in no place to say anything, so neither of us mentions it this time.

I am still vaguely feeling the MDMA when I text Sabine:

Me: *How was your night?*
S: *Cozy as a baby's ass. How was yours?*
Me: *Fun. Where are you?*
S: *House to myself. Naked except for pink silk robe in the backyard, smoking a J.*
Me: *Maybe I'll come hang? Feeling social still. Yoga?*
S: *Yes it's a beautiful walk especially if you take the back roads. We can do acroyoga. I can fly you.*

Wearing headphones in my ears, I walk to where Sabine is house sitting. I am surprised to see the outside of the house is the same color paint as The Aquarium.

Sabine is in the kitchen, smoking weed, cleaning the stove, making hard-boiled eggs. She is listening to music on her computer. She pours out more MDMA on the laptop. I lick my finger, letting the drug melt on my tongue. I sing along with Coco Rosie. Sabine reads me an essay she wrote called *Dominance and Submission.* She looks so sweet sitting there in the sun, or maybe it's the drugs, but I keep snapping photos of her.

Sabine tells me to go lie down in the kid's room, where there's a colorful carpet and toys. I do Upward-Facing Dog and moan from pleasure and then lie on my stomach. Sabine walks over and lies on top of me. We stay like that and talk for a while until one of us says, *Let's take a bath.* I go into the bathroom and remove my clothes. I take naked photos of myself with my phone while listening to Sabine bang around in the kitchen. She walks into the bathroom with two plates holding open-faced egg salad sandwiches. *You're the funniest person*, I say. *Egg salad in the bathtub, who does that?* She's even garnished it with arugula.

She stands next to me and we take more photos. Our hips are the same height, our belly buttons, and breasts. I think of sending a photo to Finn but don't want to upset her. (I tiptoe around her state of mind, cave to her jealousies, try to protect her.) I take some bites of my sandwich, then climb into the tub. The MDMA is kicking in, stunting my appetite. My head tingles.

This is the first time as an adult that I have bathed with another person. There is something about Sabine that makes me feel simultaneously powerful and relaxed. Safe.

With Finn, I can trick myself into feeling safe, emotionally, but it's exactly that – a trick.

When we get out of the bath we are shivering. *Do you have anything cozy to wear?* I ask her. *I have a poncho*, she says. I wear her black and yellow poncho all day.

We get into bed – a pulled-out futon with red sheets. The curtains are also red, the sun peeking around the edges. We smoke weed and listen to Grimes. On drugs, I am talking about the movies *Pocahontas* and *E.T.*

I remember thinking I would never have done this with Sabine if I hadn't done it first with Finn. I felt I was out of my comfort zone, that this was not my real life, it was my life enhanced, a movie scene, and I was looking down at myself from above, saying, *Who are you?*

Do you want to be flogged? Do you know what that is? Sabine asks.

I think so, I say. *It's when you stick something up someone's ass?*

Nooooooo, she laughs. *It's where I do sexual healing on you, and release your energy.*

She presents a feathered whip from her bag, and I lie on my stomach with my pants on but no shirt. She straddles me and lightly tickles my back with the whip. After, we nap and when we wake Sabine says, *I need to masturbate.* I have never masturbated with another person but around Sabine I do not feel self-conscious. I masturbate on my stomach and she on her back. I come first. Sabine takes much longer. When she is getting close, she asks me to choke her and to look in her eyes and I comply. I remember thinking Finn would not believe what kind of day I am having. And also that she would never understand.

It's six p.m. when we make it out of the bedroom and into the glittering sunlight. We sit on the hammock together on the porch of the ocean-colored house. Sabine smokes a joint, and I tell her about Finn. *Men are simple, they just want sex. It's the women we should be afraid of,* she says.

Sabine makes us dinner while I read her some of Finn's emails. Sabine asks if I will sleep with her for the night. I do. I sleep clothed and Sabine sleeps naked – the opposite of Finn and I. I tell Sabine that I know Finn and I need to stop seeing one another. That it's wrecking me. That I must grieve it, but that I don't want to let go. *What color and heat do you see when you grieve?* she asks, while lightly touching my face. *Blue*, I say. *I like how you touch me differently when you talk about her*, she says. *I do? How?* I ask. *Way more aggressively*, she says.

Finn and I both have a birthday in spring. She gives me nothing for my birthday; I give her nothing for hers. On my birthday eve, Nathan and I hit the bars after work. We drink 'white trashes' (shit whiskey followed by Miller High Life) and at the end of the night we find ourselves at a strip club. I keep putting dollar bills into the strippers' underwear and a man on the loudspeaker says, *Please don't touch the dancers*. Nathan drives me home and is patient with my manic chatter while we sit parked outside The Aquarium. I sing along to 'Dream On' by Aerosmith and when I'm finished, I lean over and vomit on the sidewalk. Nathan holds my hair back from my face, rubs my back. When I finish he looks apologetic and embarrassed. He tells me he's gotten his period and could he come use the bathroom. His testosterone levels are out of whack. I feel terrible that he's been silently struggling all night. We walk downstairs to The Aquarium and he gently points out to me that I have pissed myself.

I wake up hungover on my birthday, call a cab to get me to the library on time. I leave the house with my high-heeled, lace-up boots untied and when I get into the cab the driver says, *You live dangerously*. Finn stops in to see me at work.

She tells me it's my last year before I am an adult. Or maybe that I am an adult now. I forget. After she leaves she emails me to say she loves my shirt. *It's a great birthday shirt*, she says.

I am upset, irritated that I cannot go out with Finn on my birthday. I distract myself with other friends, go for dinner and drinks with them. During the dinner Finn emails me, texts me, tweets at me, reviews one of my books on Goodreads. I ignore her until I get home. Then I respond to everything.

I do not see Finn on her birthday. She is in Costa Rica with her girlfriend. Instead I go cold, ignore her texts and emails.

At the library, I can look up what books Finn has borrowed. I always know what she's reading. I check every day when I get to work. I tell her I do this and she laughs and says, *I'm gonna start borrowing certain books as messages to you*. She checks out *A Lover's Discourse* by Roland Barthes and Batman comics. She reads bestselling novels and tons of poetry and critical essays and crime fiction. She reviews everything she reads on Goodreads. She has me read the novel *Stone Butch Blues* by Leslie Feinberg so I'll understand her better. It's in this book that I learn the terms 'stone butch' and 'stone femme' and learn at least a little about the way her mind works. Finn admits that she feels like she has a cage around her. She says she wants the cage to come down. I learn there are books like S. Bear Bergman's *Butch is a Noun*, which explains: *Toughness, even at the expense of gentleness, is a butch trait. Butches are outlaws. Also gentlemen. Gentlemen who open doors and pick up checks and say 'after you' and hold your umbrella over you in the rain while the water drips down their sleeves. Butches are always tops, they always fuck the girls and for that matter their partners are always girls; there is no such thing as a butch who is attracted to men.*

She tells me about the novel *Annie On My Mind* and the movie *Loving Annabelle* and the shows *Lip Service* and *The L Word*. She tells me about the movie *If These Walls Could Talk*. There is so much out there I don't know, never knew, have to learn, will never understand.

My mom's birthday also falls during spring and she flies in to visit me. I meet her at the airport. I do with my mother many of the same things I do with Finn. We lie in my bed in The Aquarium and watch films. My mom sleeps on the side of the bed Finn slept on. I get dressed with my mom still in the room; she makes comments on my outfit choices. I have a newfound fascination with my mother – if she has a new bracelet, I want to try it on. If she has a glass of water, I want a sip. If she has boots I haven't seen, I want to borrow them for the day. I want to know her dreams in the morning. It was similar with Finn: I'd take her hat off of her head and put it on my own. I took her rings off of her fingers and onto my own. I once told her I wanted to dress up in all her clothes. When she is chewing gum, I ask for a piece. If she's getting a second coffee, I want one too. If she loves a book she is reading, I will read the same book. I wanted what was not mine.

Though I've always felt affectionate with my mom, I feel it more acutely now. Taking her hand under the table at bars. Noticing whether or not she touches me during the night while we sleep or rubs my back in the morning. She left me a voicemail after I moved away that said, *I miss you! I don't see you or hug you or touch you enough!* As an early childhood teacher, my mom has always known the importance of touch.

Over the years, I noticed I was closer with my mom than my girlfriends were with theirs. When I sleep at my mom's house, I sleep with her in her bed instead of my childhood one. When I was a child, until age seven, we showered together. I watched her dress, observing the softness of her body, the swell of her breasts. During puberty, excited about the changes in my own body, I'd say, *Mom look!* and show her the new hair I'd found, the way my breasts were expanding. We'd nap together. Hold hands. At family events into my early twenties, I would sit on her lap.

I cannot find a word for how I feel about my mother. One night while we lie in bed, we make shadow puppets on the wall. We have laughing fits. In the morning, sitting on the stoop, drinking our coffee, I read our horoscope aloud. (I read Finn's horoscope silently. When I admitted once to Finn that I read her horoscope each month in the newspaper, she replied that she reads my daily horoscope online, to navigate my moods.)

The day of her birthday, my mom and I sleep in late. It's the last day of her visit and we're tired from waiting for the bus and walking all the time. It's a gloomy, bleak morning. I wake up depressed. She asks me about Finn and I tell her I cannot talk about it yet. She prods and pushes but I can't get the words out. My arm is covering my face. She gives up and leaves the bed. While my mother showers, I lie in bed listening to the rain. I am filled with regret; I wish I could talk. I want to tell my mother everything. But I worry that if I begin crying, I will never stop. I will never get out of bed. If my mother gives me sympathy, I worry I will collapse, get on the plane home with her.

The first three times I drafted this piece, I omitted Finn's girlfriend from the manuscript. I was afraid of how her inclusion would make me look: irresponsible, unethical, careless, selfish, bad. Of how it would make Finn look the same. I don't know why I thought it was my job to protect Finn. When I talked to Dr. Kay about this, she told me Finn had never been my friend. She told me I couldn't see the situation back then. That my hand was right up to my nose and I couldn't see it, couldn't see past it. And yet, I still feel ashamed for hurting Finn.

During lunch with an editor, he told me that to write fiction, I should just make the situation go the way I want it to go. So I tried leaving Finn's girlfriend out of the manuscript. But it didn't make sense this way. Early readers didn't understand where all the drama was coming from. Finn and I rarely talked about her girlfriend. Instead, we allowed her to be a looming tempest around everything we did.

It took me several drafts to include her, even here on the page. I never even give her a name. I can only refer to her as 'Finn's partner' or 'Finn's girlfriend' in that way you refer to anyone you feel uncomfortable referring to directly.

Even when we'd been just friends, Finn had seldom mentioned her girlfriend, and when she did so, it was either in a neutral or negative manner, depending on her mood. Sometimes she'd make small comments about something they had done together, to remind me, I thought, of her ongoing situation. She often missed my readings because she didn't want her girlfriend to come to them with her and she couldn't come without her. Her girlfriend was not on Twitter, and so Finn and I used Twitter as our main form of public communication. Both of them were on Facebook, however, and there were times I spent hours looking at their shared photographs. Later, after Finn and I had stopped talking, I deactivated my account, preferring not to see them.

I can't see you anymore, I tell Finn one night when the darkness of the situation hits me, the way it usually does when I am drinking. I am in bed and she is standing at the door, peeking outside to make sure there is no ticket on her car. Always the comedian, she replies: *Do you want me to turn on the light?* I tell her she isn't funny. (She will mock me on the phone the next day, make fun of how mad I was, of the way I said, *You're not funny.* She will say, *Last night was dark. You were dark.*) When she finishes her jokes, she climbs back in bed with me. I am facing the wall. I say, *I need to change the way I live my life.* She says yeah, or she says nothing. I do not remember.

I don't, of course. Of course I don't change my life. Not yet anyway. Instead, I meet her in bars. There is no schedule to our madness. I never know which nights or weekends I will see her. Everything is arranged last minute, as it is in affairs, because that is what we are having, even if I don't want to think of it in this way. I often think of it as *the situation*, but we are *having an affair*. We sit on barstools, almost touching but not quite. Knees close. Mouths close. We are trying to resist one another, enjoying the suspense. We both know what is going to happen but we pretend otherwise. We talk about our families. Our siblings. Our parents dying. How worried we are about the future. She tells me her coming-out story. She tells me she likes what I am wearing. She asks nuanced questions, references to tiny admissions she remembers me saying in the past – *Do you still sing? Do you miss your hometown? Where in Europe have you been? Are you feeling good being off drugs? How long has it been?* I am dressed up, often buying new garments before I see her. I wear lacey dresses, new bras, I straighten my hair; I put on a full-face of makeup. I purchase a bra the same color blue as The Aquarium. Before I'd left to meet her, I met my face in the mirror, and was shocked. I am taking an array of vitamins, sort of compulsively, trying to keep my mood balanced, and

I think they give me different side effects. My pupils are the largest they will ever be.

Even in a sweatshirt, she is never not dapperly dressed, trim, and handsome. Her clothes look, smell, and feel clean. They look ironed. She calls herself vain. We barhop. We get slices of pizza. While we walk from bar to bar, passing groups of men, some of whom make comments to us, others who remain silent, she mutters angry threats. *I'll kill you*, she mumbles. She tells me she is always thinking about how she will jump the people around her.

The last bar of the night has a leather couch in the back of the room that is vacant. While she grabs it I go to the bar, order her a cocktail, myself a tequila shot. It is unusual for her to allow me to pay. I am conscious of enjoying this reversal of roles. I am aware of her watching me as I stand at the bar.

Finn and I people-watch from the couch. We talk about our 'types.' I ask her what her type is and she immediately says, *Girly.* Then she goes on to describe me, jokingly. Then she says: *Portia.* She strips her layers off until she is wearing a black T-shirt. She's leaning back against the couch. She says, *I feel like I wanna smoke a cigarette.* I love when she loosens up like this, but it takes me so long to get her to this place. She looks at me looking at her, and says, *In my wildest dreams, I never thought you would look at me that way.* I ask her if she thinks I will end up with a man or a woman and very quickly she replies, *Man.* She does not hesitate.

Later, after we'd stopped seeing each other, friends asked me why she wasn't worried about being in public with me, being seen with me, why she didn't worry someone might say something to her girlfriend. I can't speak for her, but I can say, it depended on her mood. Yes, she worried. She was constantly worried, but she also had a great capacity to push her worries aside, and to be a performer. She had a knack for acting, for pretending everything was normal. We both did. Why couldn't two females go for drinks together? That's what we did before we'd been sexual. Though, the one time we did run into a mutual friend, someone who knew both Finn and her girlfriend, she did not introduce me.

I have meditated repeatedly on what it was about Finn that had me so dismantled. Looking back, I see she mirrored me. She listened. I would say something to her and she would paraphrase it back to me. This made me feel understood, something she could *see* I craved. She was chivalrous. She was emotionally available (even when she was not).

My ex-boyfriend emails me, *Great lovers are hard to find. It's all about touch and smell.* He and I had that, and since him, I'd had it with no one until Finn. The thought of her made me nuts, would have me masturbating on my bedroom floor. When I dated men, I held back. Once, an ex-boyfriend said to me, irritated, *You like, emailed me twice today.* Twice! Finn and I could easily break over seventy-five emails daily. Back and forth, back and forth. Banter and proclamations of love and compliments and general worries of the future. We write how lucky we are that we found each other, have each other. *I don't know what it is*, she says, *but our minds click. We're mind clickers.*

A few months into my relationship with Finn, I get into a trivial argument with a childhood friend. She is living in a different city, so we leave each other voicemails, long streams of texts. Admittedly, I'm more upset than she is. After one of my long-winded texts, she writes back, *Wow, you're so dramatic.* This stops me for a moment and I feel embarrassed, called out on something. She is right. I have become much more dramatic while involved with Finn. I think this is partly because Finn is in a relationship (with someone who is not me), but also because Finn engages in the drama. Months before that, Finn and I are emailing back and forth, incredibly dramatic tones. *We are soooo dramatic sometimes*, I told her. She wrote back, *Lol, SOOOO. Someday we'll read these out loud together and make fun of ourselves.*

While writing this book, I live in a different city, hundreds of miles from Finn. I spend the better part of my day writing. I take long walks in the afternoon. At night I read or listen to podcasts. I replace my own words with others. Sometimes, in the evening, I sit at the kitchen table with my roommate, a poet. We sip on wine or tea, talk about being female writers. About bi-curiosity and past relationships. Eventually I tell her about Finn. I tell her what I have told you, that she made me feel special, that she complimented me. No, my roommate says. She says it cannot be just that. She says there is something else. Something chemical. Mysterious. She goes as far as to use the word *mystical*. She says she bets other people have complimented me, but coming from them it did not mean as much to me. I go to bed that night repeating the word *mystical* in my head. It reminds me of something I read once. The writer was explaining how when a certain lover does something – that makes you nuts, whatever that may be – they bite your ear or say a certain dirty word or kiss a particular part of your body, it means everything, gets you off. But when you ask another lover to do the same exact thing, it has no meaning, no effect. You are unmoved.

When I first began writing these anecdotes about my grief, it was while I was still seeing Finn. I wrote in short bursts, not focusing or concentrating, more like taking notes. I'd asked Finn if she wanted to see them. *Not yet*, she said. *It's too soon.* Working on this book now though, it feels as though everything happened to someone else. Not me. A version of me. *As soon as you write something down, it's fiction.* (Chris Kraus said this somewhere, I forget where I read it.) In her book *The Buddhist*, Dodie Bellamy chronicles an affair she had with her spiritual teacher. Over time the Buddhist tells Bellamy he is terrified she is going to write about him. She writes: *This guy must have some self-destructive streak – he's read my writing, what was he possibly thinking?*

By summer I have stopped communicating with Finn. My life expands without her in it. My head begins to clear. The sun is magnificent; it wakes me early, and in the sun, I change. I am light and energetic. My days are spent in my backyard reading books of nonfiction. I find solace in devastating memoirs (miscarriages, natural disasters, death, and addiction). When I tell people what I'm reading, people who read fiction and not memoirs, they're usually appalled at the storyline. *How is that fun for you?* they ask. I read for hours, drinking coffee and eating toast and sweating from the brilliant sun.

I attend a Saturday morning writing class and it is there that I meet The Female Woody Allen. She is in her forties, a New Yorker, openly neurotic and the most un-politically correct person in America. She emails me a few weeks after the class and asks if I'd be interested in bartering – her cabin in the woods in exchange for some writing feedback. She deems us dark horses and we borrow each other's books. She tells me about the word *Schadenfreude*, which translates to harm-joy, the feeling of pleasure or joy derived from the misfortune of others. Of course, I am not malicious and do not wish harm on others. It's just that I love a good train wreck, possibly to distract me from my own.

In Finn's absence, I crave the attention of women. I jump at the chance to be around females, in public and private settings, with friends and strangers. I have sleepovers with Lily that we call adult slumber parties. We go to bed early, side by side, and cook breakfast leisurely in the mornings. I also join an online dating site. (*Remember when you went dyke shopping?* The Female Woody Allen asked me over the phone recently. *That sounded exhausting. And depressing!*) I am a social fucking butterfly, I accept all invitations – and often I do the inviting. One Saturday I go on three dates in a row with women I meet online.

I tell myself these dates are a distraction technique but there is a part of me that hopes I will fall in love. I meet a woman who describes herself in her online profile as 'a dyke' who 'ride bikes.' This is perfect, and I wonder if she will be like Finn. I meet her on the patio of a bar, and ten minutes into our conversation I learn: 1) she's an alcoholic, 2) Augusten Burroughs is her hero, 3) she checks herself into rehab often. She works delivering sandwiches for a café. Her face is all busted up from falling off of her bike the night before, drunk. I'm attracted to this kind of mess. We make plans to hang out again, and a few days later I meet her outside her grandmother's house. We sit on the lawn close to one another and she passes me the apple she is eating. I take a bite and pass it back. This feels intimate to me. Sharing saliva. *Are we girlfriends?* I wonder in my head, *Or are we just sharing an apple?* We walk to the grocery store to buy a six-pack and I make a salad at the salad bar. She asks me for ten dollars to purchase the beer, saying she doesn't have any money. She whispers in my ear, *Just walk out the door with the salad.* I am surprised when she says this, not because it's something I have never done, but because it is something I *have*.

We sit outside drinking beers, sharing my stolen salad, which is when she tells me she was recently arrested for stealing beer from this grocery store. She tells me she had done a bag of cocaine beforehand and I start to wonder about the recklessness of hanging out with a girl like this. I descend forward through the day with her, anyway. On some level I know I should feel uncomfortable, but I do not, and when she says, *Follow me*, I do. I follow her through her bedroom window. We lie in her bed, drink Svedka, and play with her cat and don't have sex, though I keep wondering if we will. She gives me a tiny bag of cocaine and I put it in my pocket. She says she has to go meet a friend at the park and do I want to come? I say no. I've had enough for one day. Instead, I sit on the lawn outside her grandmother's house with the cocaine in my pocket. Eventually I walk home and snort the cocaine, which is anti-climactic. I never see her again.

Another woman sends me an enthusiastic and articulate message about books and writing because in my profile I say I am a writer. We meet late one night at a bar. She wears a blazer and glasses. She is from Ireland. Her profile says that one of the first things people notice about her is that she's androgynous. She's tall and skinny and blonde and feminine. She says she is *the gayest person in the world* but in my head I think, *I've seen gayer.* She's five years younger than I am. Ten inches taller. She walks me home. We go on a few more dates – to the movies, to dinner and drinks, and to a show. She pays for everything. She has money and a car; I have nothing. One night after she drops me off at The Aquarium, she texts me, *Come outside.* I am apprehensive and it is raining but I go out anyway. She is already standing there, waiting for me. She says, *I just need to know for myself is this is heading toward romantic for you, or if it's platonic.* I tell her I don't know. I say, *Can I think about it?* She says, *I'm disappointed, but not really surprised. You always seemed hesitant.* We stay friends, drive to the beach, grab drinks, go dancing. Months later I receive a mass email from her with the subject line 'Gender!' Those of us who receive this email are to know she now identifies as 'Genderqueer' and we must try to transition away from the pronouns 'she' and 'her.'

A friend sets me up with a woman named Angel. Angel is wearing the uniform of women our age in this city – American Apparel sweatshirt under a jean jacket, black jeans, and Frye boots. They are the Motorcycle design. She is sure to tell me she actually used to *ride* a motorcycle and that's why she has them. We run into a group of her friends and she begins telling them about a girl she met and is falling in love with. *She's thirty, which is perfect.* She turns to me and says, *No offense, but I really need a partner who has already gone through the Saturn Return.* We finish our 'date' and I go back home to my basement where I watch movie trailers repeatedly and listen to songs about unrequited love.

I meet another girl on a patio of a bar. Her posture is horrendous and her social skills nonexistent. I find out she is a vegan, and ask her related questions until I excuse myself, saying I have to go to a friend's house to meet her new dog.

I find a profile that intrigues me. The woman labels herself 'bisexual' and I like the way she looks in her photo, short curly hair and flawless skin. We meet at a tea shop and it goes smoothly; we talk for a couple of hours. She drives me home. Afterwards, I feel hopeful about her, like it's possible we will start dating. Later she texts me to ask if I want to fly a kite on our next date and I lose interest. We decide we'll go to a movie instead. It takes us a while to decide on a film – I want to see something indie, she does not. We compromise and see a comedy. Sitting in the front row, craning our necks, she says, *Sorry if it seems like I'm in a weird mood. Today my friend told me that she and none of our friends enjoy my company.* I have no idea how to respond. I have wine with The Female Woody Allen that night and we look up my date on Google images. We discover she is a pretty well-known female musician in this town. *She thinks she's Ani DiFranco,* The Female Woody Allen says.

There is a café I go to in the morning because a lesbian who reminds me of Finn works there. She has a buzzed haircut, a chain wallet, baggy jeans and bound breasts. I sit at the counter, drinking coffee and reading. She never lets my coffee cup get empty. She notices I am reading *Stone Butch Blues. I read that a million years ago*, she says. I try to find the courage to ask her if she wants to get a drink after her shift, but I can't bring myself to do it.

I wake early one morning, and walk around outside before the café opens. I am drinking seltzer from a can and when she comes outside she says, *I thought you were out here drinking a beer.* She lets me in and I order a coffee and an egg and cheese sandwich. I sit at the counter and read my horoscope and then Finn's. When she hands me my to-go bag, she smacks her forehead, realizing she's given me the wrong kind of cheese. I tell her it's not a big deal, really, but she seems so embarrassed that I never go back.

One Saturday morning I visit a farmers' market. I walk aimlessly around, hungry but not knowing what to buy, feeling indecisive, sampling apple slices and berries. As I approach a booth selling goat milk cheese and loaves of bread, a shorthaired woman with dark skin and a beanie makes eye contact with me. I say hi to her. She asks me if I like hot sauce. She hands me a sample of sauerkraut. I tell her I'm starving; I forgot to eat today. Before I walk away she says, *Wait. Here take this*, and hands me a napkin filled with flax and raisin bread samples. In my delusional state, I wonder if this woman wants to sleep with me, and plan on going back to the farmers' market next weekend, though I end up forgetting.

I stare at women, catching myself turning around to look at their asses and their legs. I don't fully realize this until I move away – that my neighborhood is full of lesbians. They wear a uniform of black jeans, boots and dark denim jackets. I have gotten used to them in my peripheral. At the library, I notice more gay female couples than I have in my whole life. I gawk at them. I try to figure out which one does the fucking and then I imagine them fucking. Only once do I see another 'sweet spot' girl. I text this to Finn even though we are not speaking and Finn says she will have to kill her.

Growing up, I had a tight-knit group of male friends. My parents divorced when I was twelve, and that same year my two best girlfriends transferred to private schools. This left me with three best male friends. They were my support system. They knew they were part of a dark time, even if we didn't speak of it much. My dad had just moved out. I slept next to them, the three of us on the pullout couch with me in the middle. There was nothing sexual between us. Curiosity, maybe, but nothing was acted on. I was not grossed out by their perverse sense of humor and could keep up with their high energy. We liked the same music; my mom drove us to concerts. We saw dozens of movies. Now though, in this city, I am rarely around males. My closest friend is Nathan, and even he was once a woman.

I email a friend I grew up with and ask her if she thought I was more interested in females than males in high school. I am grasping at my identity. I am questioning everything, especially my past. *It never really seemed like you were interested in guys*, she answers, *they seemed like more of a convenience thing to you. And when you had one best girl friend you neglected all the rest.* I've had so many close female friends, but I don't remember feeling *in love* with them. Though the friendships verged on unhealthy and codependent. The men I've loved most have been effeminate, sensitive, and flamboyant. The man I was most intimate with for years calls me and I tell him I've fallen in love with a woman. I tell him I am preferring women to men. I ask him if he is surprised by this. *No*, he says. *Of course you are. Men are like hairy rocks, but women! Women are like soft magical fairies!*

I have a memory of texting Isaac: *I wish I were bisexual. I feel I am missing out. Yeah*, he responded, *it's like double the sex*.

We begin seeing each other again a month after our break-up. Finn is angry about the way in which I stopped communicating with her, abruptly, without explanation. *Never do that again without telling me first*, she says. She takes my hand, holds it up next to hers and we compare colors. *You're tan – whatchu been doing, reading outside?* I nod. (In my head I think, *How did she know?*)

We spend the night together, and in the morning when we wake, we silently look at each other on our pillows, half a face each. One eye and eyebrow. She extends her arm across the bed to me and I extend mine to her, so our hands rest in the crook of each other's elbows. I am laughing for no reason, or maybe because I merely feel happy. *Why you laughin' at me?* she says, and then, *Stop laughin' at me. I'm fragile.* She comes toward me and puts her head on my chest. I am wearing her '*Drugs*' shirt again. She tugs on the sleeve of the shirt and mumbles, I *was gonna give you this for your birthday, but I thought that would be weird.*

I smile and say, *You know what I like about you?*

No, what? she says.

You're romantic.

I think I'm depressing, she sighs.

Later that day, sitting half dressed in my bra and tights on Finn's bed, I listen to k.d. lang on my phone while she showers. *I thought I heard music*, she says, entering the room. She grabs my head and kisses me hard. *One, two, or three?* she asks, standing at my back. What? Oh. She is talking about the clasp on my bra. It is undone and she is asking me which clasp she should put it on, one, two, or three? I tell her I don't know. Any of them are fine. Maybe two. I'm not sure. No one has ever asked me this before.

I buy a pair of shoes at a thrift store that are not my style. *Like my shoes?* I ask a co-worker. *Pretty butch*, he says. I take a photo of myself wearing a T-shirt and jeans and trucker hat and text it to Nathan. *You have never looked more dyke-y*, he responds. I buy a pair of Levis at a yard sale that are two sizes too large. They make me feel like Finn. I wonder if these jeans will help me attract women, if they will put a message out, but they just look like too-big-jeans. *Get a belt*, one of my co-workers says to me. I want to look like her. There was a time Finn said, *My clothes define me.* I was jealous of this. I did not know how to define myself through my looks. I still don't.

I begin going to events, queer dance parties. The morning of the first dance party, I wake excited. I imagine myself dancing with a woman. I imagine us going home together. That night I beg Lily to come with me. She doesn't want to pay the cover charge to enter the dance room, so we park ourselves at the bar, and I watch the lesbians enter, showing their IDs to the bouncer. I suck my ginger ale through a straw and eyeball them. The theme of the night is *Brokeback Mountain*, and they all look disturbingly sexy to me, in their flannels and wife-beaters, cut-off shorts, and freshly trimmed haircuts. Lily and I go outside to the patio. We are surrounded by dozens, maybe a hundred, females. I'm overwhelmed. That night, I know the definition of yearning. I feel invisible. *See me! Help me! I am hurting! Make me feel good. Someone who looks like you has put an ache in my heart.*

Things hurt worse before they hurt better. We stop talking without talking about it. My therapist has me draw a picture of how I'm feeling. I draw a bright yellow circle, then surround it with black and cage it in. I walk around chanting: *It's like a plane flew into your soul. It's like two planes flew into your soul* in my head, which is something I read in a Junot Diaz story. I feel inside out. Warped. Sorrow leaks from my skin. I inhale chocolate bars in bed. The caffeine doesn't keep me up. My ex-boyfriend's mother dies of AIDS. I double over in grief. He calls me every day and yet I never expect the call. We talk anywhere from two to five hours a day. He is walking around Chinatown in New York City. I am sitting in my backyard outside The Aquarium ripping grass out of the ground. He tells me his life is an episode of *Six Feet Under*. At the library I sneak into the bathroom stall to answer his calls. We take turns listening to each other cry. My friend who is out of town calls and asks me to euthanize her cat. I drive to the Humane Society on a bright and balmy morning, blasting Leonard Cohen on the way, drowning out the sounds of the crying cat. In the office, the vet asks me if I want a few minutes alone with the cat, to say goodbye. I shake my head no, walk into a corner of the room, clutching my stomach and mouth, swallowing sobs. The Female Woody Allen offers me her cabin in the woods for a weekend. Lily drives us in her truck, and I sit passenger, my feet on the dashboard, windows down. When we arrive and unlock the door, a hummingbird flies in and up to the window. The window is fifteen feet above us and we cannot find a ladder. We spend the better part of the day brainstorming ways to save the bird. The hummingbird is female, with her white throat. In late afternoon we climb the ladder to the loft bed. We read for a while and Lily falls asleep. I lie next to her listening to her breathe and the bird buzz and smack into the window. ZzzzzzzzzSMACK. ZzzzzzzSMACK. She tries the same method over and over. *Try a new way!* I shout in my head.

During my break at the library, I open *The Book of Questions*. I open randomly to a page and the question is: 'Would you exclude sex from your life for a year if you knew you'd be more peaceful?'

I sign up for a five-week writing class and only go to the first two. I sign up to four weeks of philosophy of yoga class and go to zero. I find myself walking around the mall. I purchase clothes and return them the next day. I eat soft pretzels and drink smoothies from Jamba Juice. I lurk around the gender and queer studies section at bookstores. I buy anthologies about women coming out of the closet and leave them on the coffee table. In the mornings I masturbate repeatedly.

Lily has this therapist she raves about. I want to try him out, but he lives in the South, so we do our session over Skype. He holds his hands parallel to each other, like he is praying, an inch empty space between them. *This is what healthy intimacy looks like*, he says. *But people don't know that*. He leans one hand toward the other and collapses both hands to the left. Then to the right. Like a seesaw. He explains that's what Finn and I are doing. One person gets too intimate and the other gets scared and leans away and then vice versa. And so on.

In her book *Shape of Blue*, author Liz Scheid says, *To obsess is to think about something relentlessly. A thought becomes an obsession when it takes over all other thoughts. It haunts. Dwells. Dominates. Distracts us from unwanted emotions. There is a question as to what is conscious here – do we choose it or does it choose us?* I read a *New York Times* review of a memoir that says something like, 'The author claims to be "obsessed" with [such and such]. Remember when humans were just interested in things?' On his podcast I hear Marc Maron talk about addiction, explaining it's only addiction when it hurts your life.

Finn and I weren't just interested in each other.

Finn asked me to marry her once. She was off to get our third round of drinks and she leaned over me where I was sitting. Her arm hung over the booth. She hunched over me. She told me she'd been thinking about it. *Would you marry me?* she asked. I wouldn't answer but she wouldn't let me off the hook so finally I said either *duh* or *of course.* In the morning, I reminded her of it. *What a jackass*, she said. I see now that she said, *would you*, as opposed to: *will you.*

She breaks the silence, emails and says, *You are ALL I think about. And I am trying to figure that out.* We make plans for Friday. We both have to work. She is running an errand near my library so says to meet her in the fiction aisle 'Y.' We have not seen each other in some weeks and I text her, *I'll be the one in the blue T-shirt, in case you've forgotten what I look like.* She responds, *Today I look like I'm working on the railroad.* As I walk through the library, my heart beats nervously. My hands feel clammy. I find her; her back is to me. We stand in the aisle for a moment, talking about books. We are standing close enough that the back of her hand gently grazes mine, making me light-headed. As I walk with her to the exit, she says, *So are we hanging out tonight or what?* I say, *Yes, duh*, and she smiles. As she leaves the library, she holds my eye until she gets all the way to the door. I work my shift restlessly. I email her, *ha*. She emails back, *ha, ha*.

Before she comes to The Aquarium, Finn goes to get a haircut and I drink beers with Lily in my backyard and wait for her. An hour later she joins us at the picnic table. I pretend I am her girlfriend as I walk in heels from the kitchen to bring her a Rolling Rock. Lily turns to me and says, *That night you smashed your phone on the street, I thought, maybe this person is truly crazy*, and Finn says, *Yeah, well, the jury's still out*, and we all laugh. Later Finn says, *It was fun to have that intimate buzz in front of other people.*

Lily goes home and Finn and I walk a few blocks to a bar. We link arms while we walk. At the bar, we sit next to each other on a bench on the patio. She fixes my bra that is twisted. She fixes the chain of my necklace that is twisted. She kisses my shoulder. I put one leg onto her lap. She plays with my shoe, straightens it. She asks me for the origin stories of the jewelry I am wearing. She moves my hair to see if I am wearing earrings. We don't know when the first kiss will come and we draw it out until we can't take it anymore. *We're so good at this*, she says. She orders me a grilled cheese I barely touch.

I tell Finn about my online dates. *Oh no, don't tell me you have an Ok Cupid profile, cause now I'm gonna have to go look at it!* she says. We laugh at the stories. She says she is laughing because the stories remind her of herself when she was my age. I tell her about the drugs the Augusten Burroughs-lover had. *If you and I were together, I wouldn't let you do that*, she says. *Yeah, well that's never going to happen*, I say. *How do you know?* she asks. In The Aquarium that night, Finn unbuttons the shirt I am wearing, says – *wait right there!* She runs out to her car and back in with the *I Don't Do Drugs I Am Drugs* shirt and puts it over my head. I keep it on for the next two days.

Maybe we made a mistake tonight, I say. She knows exactly what I mean but instead says, *Yeah, I agree, we should have skipped the bar and stayed in The Aquarium together all night.*

She belly-flops on my bed and says things like, *What if I'm in love with you? Are you afraid I'm going to tell you what you want to hear? Or what you don't want to hear?* I answer, *Both.* She repeats it: *Both.* She says she wants to move out of her apartment, but not for me, for herself. She says that when she has her own apartment, I can come over. She wants to make me macaroni and cheese at night. She wants to eat cereal with me in the morning. I put my fingers in my ears and say *lalalalalala* because I know it won't happen and I don't want to be devastated when it doesn't. She says I never believed in her. She says she thinks it would be worth it to leave her relationship even if she could only have me for six months. *Why six months?* I ask her. *Because I don't think you'll stay*, she says, and we both go quiet.

There's an undertone of sadness to the night. I say, *I don't understand why you're here, it confuses me.* She says she wanted to see me. She wanted to make sure I was okay. *Do you want me to leave?* No. Yes. No. Yes. Of course I want you to leave. Of course I don't want you to leave.

When she tells me she loves me, I pretend I cannot hear her. *What?*

She asks if she can take a naked picture of me. She asks like I'm going to say no, like it's a bad thing to ask. *Right now?* I say. *No just, sometime*, she says. *Sure*, I say.

It's time for her to go. It's four in the morning. She tucks me in. *Turn off my light*, I demand. *Turn off my light*, she repeats, mocking me. *Stop mocking me*, I say. *Stop mocking me*, she repeats. She walks over to the lamp on the nightstand and switches it off. She collects her keys and handkerchief and phone from the dresser. She stands in the doorway and says we'll go shopping soon for handcuffs and a vibrator. *We'll go together*, she says, *Saturday*. I tell her I cannot go Saturday. My mom will be in town. *Next Saturday then*, she says. She shuts the door to my bedroom. I listen to her walk up the stairs from The Aquarium and out to her car. I listen to her start her car and drive away.

We will never go through with these plans we have for the future. We will never go shopping. I think we both knew we would never go shopping. She never takes a nude photograph of me.

We never have sex again either. I don't think either of us wanted to know this.

Mania hits me hard the next morning. My heart is beating rapidly. My eyes pop open at six a.m. and I jolt out of bed. I think I have a duty. To what? I can't find my computer. Finn has put it on a shelf underneath my nightstand – I send Finn long-winded emails about my confusion. I meet Nathan for breakfast at a greasy spoon, then drive with him to Ikea where I walk around talking loudly. I cry on the drive back. *I want to leave this city*, I say. Nathan rubs my neck. He drops me off at a park. I call people. For days, I am on the phone, pacing in the sun, sitting on other people's stoops. I go into bars and order beers. I trade the beers back for wine. I lose my appetite. I am aware of how garrulous I am, but unable to stop. It's beyond my control. If I don't talk, I will disappear.

I accuse Finn through voicemail and email and text of manipulating me, of having an agenda. She freaks out at this, and says she did not manipulate me, she *fell* for me. I tell her I need to get out. She says, *You're right, you need to get out. I see this do horrible things to you, your moods, and your mental health.* I send Dr. Kay an email that I need to go on drugs, even though I know she doesn't believe in them. I tell her I am afraid of my own capacity for recklessness, self-destruction. Afraid that I seek it out, these subterranean lifestyles. Afraid of my wayward choices.

Mid-manic episode, I walk a couple miles to Lily's apartment and collapse into fetal position on her couch. I tell her I want to go on Lithium. We are barefoot and on couches across from each other. My head at her feet, her feet at my head. I burst into tears; she calls me honey. I stay for hours until I have calmed down. The next morning she calls me and asks if I want to go on a hike. We climb to the top of a mountain to see a waterfall, neither one of us speaking of Finn. I ask her how I can feel better and she says, *Comedy and roller skating.* That night, Lily emails me a photograph she took of me in front of the waterfall. I'm sort of taken aback to see that I look healthy and young, nothing like the wretchedness I feel on the inside.

Somewhere along the way, Finn and I have switched roles. I force her to kiss me in public one day downtown, and she says, *You're so aggressive!* She tells me she feels scared of me and that I make her want to vomit. I reply that I feel scared of her and that she also makes me want to vomit.

I have turned into the opposite of whatever it was she thought she was in love with. I am no fun. I am serious. I am feral, ready to pounce on her. I pounce using email, text. I am reactive. I buy coffee at the café she does. I buy fruit at the deli she does. She makes such an art of avoiding me that I want to ruin her carefully laid plan, to prove to her she does not control the universe. I walk the long way to work so that I'm able to walk by her library. It makes me nervous, and one morning I drop my smartphone on the cement, cracking the screen. I walk around with my fists curled tightly in balls, feeling combative, but no one will fight me, except myself.

Dr. Kay says that Finn and I remind her of the show *Nanny 911*. We make boundaries and don't commit to them. We tell each other we will never speak again, but we always do. I tell Dr. Kay that I am having a difficult time accepting that someone who made me feel so good could make me feel so bad. I feel stupid. I feel like such a slow learner. It takes me so long to realize that the distance between Finn's words and her actions is infinite. I feel old. I judge myself. I berate myself, thinking I should have gone through something like this earlier in my life – not now.

Finn tells me, *I will never write you again. You twist my words. You hold them against me.* But she always does – we've written hundreds of times since then.

Here I am twisting her words again. Finn says I forget that words have meaning. She says I forget that they are powerful. That you can't take them back once they are out there. Finn says I have the last word on this since I am writing a book. We disagree on so many things.

On social media later that day, I see Finn has posted, *Writers. They think everything is about them.*

A few weeks later, I wake up with the flu. I have no one to take care of me, no one to call. I call in sick to the library three days in a row. Sabine comes to town to attend a wedding with her primary girlfriend and I feel low-grade jealousy. I try to rally myself and go to breakfast with Sabine. I choke down toast. We sit at an outdoor table and Sabine drinks a coffee and smokes a joint. She walks me back to The Aquarium because I'm feeling weak and need to crawl into bed. She heads off to the wedding. The following day I see she has left a track of yellow sponges through the apartment. She's cleaned my bathroom. When I see the sponges, I smile.

My mom visits and we go wine tasting through wine country. I'm in good spirits because the sun is shining directly on my face and I am drinking wine with my mother. But I do not fool her thoroughly. Walking through the vineyard, she drapes her arm around my shoulders and asks, *Does she have a good heart?* I'm stumped by this question. No one else has asked anything like this. *I think so, yes*, I say. My mother warns me, or reminds me, *Remember, she's older. She's older than you*. I tell her I know. I know that.

We've rented a car for our wine tour. Over the day we've collected bags – we have groceries, changes of clothes, books from the library, gifts and souvenirs. My mom jokes that we have everything we need, that we could drive anywhere. Take a road trip together. I know that she is kidding, but I want to believe her anyway. I want to keep my mother's undivided attention on me in the car for weeks with no other distractions.

The last three times I see Finn, we aren't having sex anymore. She calls me at midnight and I convince her to meet me for a beer. She gives me the name of a bar near her house. When I arrive, she's laughing to herself over this thing her friend Laura has said. She asked Laura if she'd slept with so-and-so, and Laura held up her middle and pointer finger and replied, 'minimal fucking.' *We did more than that, right?* I say, and we both start laughing and she nods.

We sit across from each other like when we were just friends. Finn is guarded around me. She says she likes to see me to make sure I am 'okay.' I tell her I am fine. Just fine. The song 'Leader of the Pack' is playing. *I always wanted to be this girl singing*, I tell her. *I always wanted to be the leader*, she says. Together we sing, *Nonononononononono look out look out look out look OUT!* We slide her Guinness back and forth. Eventually I ask, *Can I sit next to you?* and she nods. She stares at my chest and says, *I'm just looking at your necklace. Whose is it? I know it's not yours.* She is right. I borrowed it from Lily. She fondles my mound of key chains, and touches the silver Buddha. *Is this a penis?* she asks. *It's the Buddha*, I say. *I guess that's why I never liked Buddha*, she says.

You don't like anything, I say. *Yes I do – I like ice cream*, she counters, making her eyes wide. *Yeah, but you don't even like sprinkles*, I say.

She walks me home. I ask her to kiss me. She does, lightly on the lips and says that's all she can do. She says she cannot take how mean and manic I become afterwards. (*I don't want to be sexual with you, he said, everything gets crazy*, Anne Carson writes in *The Glass Essay*.)

I ask her if she's seen the movie *Pariah*. *No, it looked dark*, she says. *What're you scared of dark movies?* I ask. *Yes. Especially right now*, she answers.

We hug goodbye. I tell her that I read that when you hug someone, the bonding and attachment begins after three seconds. *Let's let go after two then*, she says.

On the couch across from Dr. Kay, I act out a scene from *The L Word*, in which the character Jenny Schecter tells a friend about falling in love with a woman.

In the show's companion book *The L Word: Welcome to Our Planet*, they describe Jenny's heartache at this point, her battle to deal with an identity crisis in a place still new to her. They describe her confusion as leaving her 'unmoored'.

I feel drawn to the word 'unmoored' during this time. I look it up a few times a week. I stare at the definition on my computer screen. I love the example sentence Wikipedia uses, which says, *Left unmoored, the boat gradually drifts out to sea.* It pops into my head when I wake in the mornings, while I walk the streets, wait for the bus, the train, get into cabs, eat lunch alone, and browse the shelves at the library.

If I put the words 'brilliant' and 'amazing' into my Google search engine dozens of emails from Finn will pop up. I don't dare do it.

Any discipline that ever existed flies fast out the window. Drained of mania, I become soft, gain weight. I am lethargic and the heat makes it worse. *Poor me. There's nothing so sweet as wallowing in it, is there? Wallowing is like sex for depressives,* Jeanette Winterson writes in *Written on the Body*. I get drunk and high like in high school. I smoke weed out of a can, I drink wine out of a box. I used to be more hardcore in my self-destruction, but I am back to basics now. I develop a nap habit for the first time in my life. I'm a proper hedonist. I do most things I can without getting out of bed. I buy one dollar pizza from 7-Eleven where the guy tells me it is two dollars for two slices. I hide the pizza in my purse while I walk home because no one wants to be friends with someone who eats 7-Eleven pizza.

This is what happened: I fell in love with someone I shouldn't have fallen in love with, is what Finn says, all logical and slowly when she is mad at me one night. She talks to me like I have a learning disability. I wonder if she realizes she just quoted a Buzzcocks song, but I don't say anything. I let it go. Who cares.

The beach is the first place I am able to tell the story of Finn without crying.

Some summers ago I dated a guy who I'd drive around with on back roads, stopping at different quarries and swimming holes. When my mother met him, he and I were both wearing bathing suits, in cheerful moods, on our way to swim. Later, she seemed relieved, and said she liked me being 'active' and spending time with 'upbeat' people. *I think that's the kind of person you should be with. You don't always have to be with dark souls*, she said. My mom was tired of seeing me with bipolar people, with chain cigarette smokers and guys that wore all black and brooded. When I told Finn this, she couldn't believe it. She had my legs in her lap and was stroking them. She pointed at herself in this way as if to say, *I am the darkest person there is.* Then she said, *Your legs are shaking.*

Things lose their meaning. I am bored of things having meaning. Meaning is stressful. Meaning is new-age-y. Meaning means nothing.

Hell, I see you everywhere, she once said to me. Sometimes on the street I see boys walking toward me with baggy pants and short hair and a hat but too quickly I realize they are not her. Once she told me that she saw me on the street when I first moved here. *I was obsessed with you but you didn't know it yet,* she said.

I become familiar with the cold hard ground. On a Friday night, I drink three too many glasses of wine and I call Finn. She makes no black humor jokes. It is not an erotic mess anymore, like Sabine once told me it was. The conflict and torture is not a sign of intelligence anymore, as Finn once told me it was. It is ugly. We are exhausted. Gutted. *You're too hard!* she yells at me. *Be soft*, she orders. *I'm confused*, I tell her. *I don't know what to grieve. I can't be in a relationship with anyone*, she says, *so if you have to grieve something, grieve that.* She says this strongly. She means it. When we get off the phone I am in fetal position on the bathroom floor, holding my heart, while it literally aches.

Sabine comes to visit, directly from a summer camp – one that focuses on radical honesty, equality and compassion. I give Sabine a bag of clothes I don't want anymore including the '*Drugs*' shirt. I can't wear it and having it around depresses me. Sabine wears it to bed that same night. Finn would be irritated by this; knowing this is probably why I have given Sabine the shirt.

Sabine makes me coffee with cinnamon on the stovetop in the mornings, sleeps next to me every night, touching my lower back and abdomen gently when I can't sleep because of menstrual cramps. When I get home from the library she is always home, cooking healthy meals, watering the plants, smoking spliffs.

In her book *Unmastered*, Katherine Angel says that the person who does the fucking gets less fucked up than the person who was fucked. That's my diagnosis. Books are like doctors and I am lucky to have unlimited access to them during this time. A perk of the library. I borrow anxiety and depression workbooks, binge-eating workbooks, books on codependency. I borrow tons of memoirs from the 'wellness memoir' section. It's an intimate thing, borrowing books like *Bi Lives: Bisexual Women Tell Their Stories*, having them checked out by a co-worker, someone I have to work beside the next day.

At a literary event, I run into a well-known male author who lives on the other side of the country. He's in town for his book tour. I notice he is wearing a black T-shirt that reads *Big Dyke, Oakland California*. There is chatter all around us so we can't hear each other well, and he takes me outside, away from everyone, and says he wants to hear what's going on with me. What I am working on. He was a big supporter of my first book, interviewing me and talking about it on his radio show. I feel comfortable with him, and relieved that I can tell the truth to him, and that he genuinely asked.

I tell him I have not been writing. No, I am not working on anything. I tell him about Finn. When I break to take a breath, he says, *It sounds like you're going through a really hard time.* This shocks me somehow. Coming from someone else, it is almost as though this has never occurred to me. *I sound like I'm going through a hard time?* I ask, hurt. He softens the blow a little and says something about how it seems like a confusing time for me. Then he tells me to keep paying attention to it, and keep noticing everything. He tells me it's what makes my work what it is. This makes me feel a tiny bit better. Art! I can make it into art.

Later that night someone mentions Finn's name and I burst into tears, storm out of the show, go to a shitty bar across the street, order whiskey, talk to the old men also sitting at the bar, and eventually ask the bartender to call me a cab home.

In hindsight, I see it was my decision not to let go. I didn't know how, though some days I focused completely on it: using therapy, distraction, exercise. Other days I let myself wildly grieve. Finn affects it all: every conversation I have, what I choose to wear, what books I read, what films and shows I watch. There's that Buddhist quote, *(S)He who angers you owns you.* She owned me. I allowed it. She controlled me. I knew this feeling of misery would pass, that what I needed was time, but I was impatient. *Unfortunately, we must live through the present to get to the future,* writes Hanif Kureishi in his novel *Intimacy*.

On my day off, I go to a spa and sauna resort. The website says that nudity is welcome. I show up in a bikini, then realize everyone else is naked, and peel it off. I am alone in the hot tub with two obese lesbians. An older man is lying naked on a bench. I soak in the tub half eavesdropping on the lesbian couple, but cannot hear them well. When I get too hot, I walk over to the cold showers. The old man comes and showers next to me. Even though there are explicit signs that tell us this is a quiet place and not to make conversation, the man starts to talk to me, even worse he asks me questions, so I am forced to respond. *Have I been here before? Have I tried the sauna yet?* It's not until later when I am walking home that I have the thought: *Finn is not the last person to see me naked anymore.* I feel both depressed and ecstatic about this.

My anger scares me, but it scares her more. *It scares me when you get this mad*, she says. I tell her that I want to punch her in the face. I make her cry. I bully her. I point fingers. I blame her for everything. I am full of rage and the memory of the emails I sent scares me so much I cannot go back and look at them, to tell you what they said. I remember telling her she is a sociopath. *Why did you do this?* I ask. *I wanted to be close to you and know you forever*, she says. She reminds me *we* did this. The whole *it takes two to tango* shit. She says, *I feel like you are hurting, so all you want to do is hurt me.* She says, *I have put up with so much – your tantrums, your manic behavior. I have loved you through it all. This emotional roller-coaster has got to stop. I will never again put you in a place where we end up here. Hurt, confused, angry*. She begs me to stop sending her cruel words. I can't; I don't. She says, *Trust me, I hate myself more than you ever can*. And I know it's me that I hate. I know it's me who has chosen this.

The second to last time I see Finn it is about two months after the last time we've been sexual. We meet for coffee at a café. I am late and when I get there she's leaning against her bike, playing with her phone, shaking her head. She looks annoyed with me. I've kept her waiting. We sit at a table outside. Neither of us takes off our sunglasses. I start walking inside to get our coffees and she takes out her wallet, shakes it in the air. I tell her I'll buy this round. I know how she takes her coffee and I come back out with the two mugs and sit across from her. We keep it semi light-hearted. I can tell she is consciously trying to act reserved. She is actively not doing or saying anything that might make me believe she is still interested in me. It's hot and she points out that my chest is getting burnt. We're both sweating.

The darkness surfaces; I begin asking her what happened. She tells me to stop trying to figure everything out. *You can't figure it out! Stop trying to figure it out.* When I reach across the table and touch her hand, she pulls away and says, *Keep talking and saying what you're saying, but I can't touch, I feel overemotioned.*

But what happened – what was that? I ask. *I don't understand the question*, she says, but I keep pressing and she says, *I guess we both wanted something from each other.*

But we were so close, I say. *That's what women do*, she replies. It is also during this conversation that she makes a comment such as, *If anything, I thought you were stronger than you are.*

Well, it's cool that my first was you. I'm glad it was you, I say. She seems startled that I say this, and she seems touched. And though her sunglasses are still on, I can see her eyes get sad, I can feel her stare right through me, and I can tell from the way her mouth gets small and the way she silently nods, that she is almost going to cry.

We talk on the phone a few days after the coffee shop. We agree that for six months we'd gone to another planet. *We need to get off of this planet!* I yell. Our voices raise, then become tender, we laugh. *This is damaged*, she says. *I am exhausted and so are you*, she says.

I love you forever but I don't understand you, she says. *You are the most confusing woman I have ever met.*

She used to be able to see my mind gears turning. *What?* she'd ask, seeing a certain expression on my face. *Never mind*, I'd shake my head, and she'd say, *No – tell me what you were gonna say, put your heart on my heart.* So I'd sigh and straddle her and lay my heart down and she'd say: *This is gonna be a good one.*

A week later, Finn tells me it was a generally dark year for her and that she needs to move forward. I am babysitting when I receive this email. I am sitting on the ground throwing pinecones and counting them with The Female Woody Allen's five-year-old son. I read the email on my phone, and this email hurts me, more than any of the other words that have been slung. Finding out I am part of her dark year and that I attributed to her dark year. Then I think, maybe, for a little while I was her refuge from her dark year. Until I wasn't.

I decide to hone my joy. I dance around the kitchen to Judy Garland's *Greatest Hits* on the turntable. The sun on my chest, I spin in my socks. Bruised, exhausted, and fluttering back to earth.

The last place I see Finn is the library. It is a late weekday morning and I am working the front desk, filling in for someone while they go to the bathroom. I am staring into space and there she is, staring back at me. I have made her into a cartoon character in my mind and now she is a cartoon character in real life. She is wearing a small cap and a white and green striped sweater that I've never seen. I have a new shirt on too. She holds up her hand and waves. I wave back. A few minutes later, she starts to walk toward me but at the same moment a patron approaches me to ask questions about his lost library card, so she is forced to do her transaction with one of my co-workers. She makes an exaggerated show of acting disappointed about this. When her books are borrowed, she walks over to me. We look through the books and chat for a couple of minutes. We talk about the weather. How it's cold enough that we can see our breath in the morning. Before she leaves, she holds up her hand for me to slap. A high-five. I have been reduced to a high-five. She says she will see me soon. *No you won't*, I remember thinking. The high-five makes me think of some afterschool special, where a nerdy girl has sex with the popular football player, sees him at school the next day, and he ignores her. Pretends it never happened. My mother used to say, that after sleeping with someone, you can't go back to holding hands. But can you go back to high-fiving?

She emails me twice in one hour after that interaction. She says, *Sorry about the awkward high-five. I'm a dork like that.* Then she sends me a link to a memoir she wants to read but she is afraid it will break her heart.

I don't respond immediately. She sends another email apologizing for all the emails. *Sometimes I get exuberant*, she says.

We continue to email through the fall. We say we are pen pals. We write 'Dear pen pal' at the top of the emails. She tells me she loves the perspective I have on the world. I tell her I am so glad we're finally 'just friends.' But it feels like we are doing something bad. I look forward to it too much. I stay up too late because of it. This might sound crazy, or you might know exactly what I am talking about.

Eventually it becomes obvious to me that I have stopped living and started killing time. My participation in life is slim to none. It is fair to say that engaging in some form with Finn, even when it was silence, was my hobby. Without it, I don't have much. The main source of my pleasure now comes from sleeping. I have a friend comment that I sleep more than anyone else she knows. I go to bed early; I wake up late. I sleep to escape my feelings. I can sleep twelve hours and it is not enough. At three or four p.m. in the afternoon, I begin fantasizing about sleeping. I buy the highest milligram melatonin available, to knock me out further. I buy a sleep mask. I have found a new hobby. I have tried so many routes to oblivion. Food, sex, drugs, bad relationships. So now I sleep. I rearrange my furniture so that my computer is on a dresser above my bed. I watch stand-up comedy each night while waiting for the melatonin to kick in. When I am not sleeping I am in the back row at the movies or walking around the city to go work my measly shift. I do not write, ever, the way I anticipated I would when I got the job at the library. I do not dare to write, only to read and watch television and films.

Having put all of my energies into Finn, I have lost parts of my life. I have not been thinking of my future. There has been nothing outside of my tunnel vision. It is the end of our infatuation. There are no more high highs or low lows. Emailing with Finn, having coffee with Finn, is no longer exciting. It's like when you relapse with your drug of choice after some years, and your body doesn't like it anymore. Things that sat well no longer sit well. The way you can drink whiskey in your early twenties, but later in life it comes back up your throat. What was exhilarating and rousing later makes your stomach turn.

I've been despising this city for months. I disclose this to The Female Woody Allen, and she says, *Dude what the fuck are you doing here? You're miserable. Get out of here. Go home. Get out of this one horse town and see what happens.*

Finn hears that I am leaving from a mutual friend at the library. She emails me that it's heartbreaking. *Heartbreaker. You leaving.* She says this even though we don't see each other anymore, only email.

I cannot bring all of my books home and I don't have money to ship them so I put them on street corners. My train wreck memoirs, my self-help workbooks.

My last two weeks in town are spent house sitting at The Female Woody Allen's house while she's in Amsterdam. I completely isolate myself. I give my two weeks' notice to the library. On my last day of work, I say goodbye to Nathan and simply walk out the door.

I develop a mild case of agoraphobia. I do not want to see friends, co-workers, colleagues. I cancel a reading I am supposed to do and I do not show for a close friend's book party. I avoid the libraries; take alternate routes through town. Full days pass without me saying a word. I do not pick up my phone. I attempt to make soup, stir-fry, to use up every single ingredient in the house, so I don't have to go to the grocery store. This is challenging as I cannot cook, have not cooked anything the entire year. I decline all invitations. I sleep.

Finn goes silent during this time. Even though she has written me: *Let's hang out before you go? Definitely?* multiple times. But now she ignores me. She does not respond when I tell her I am free this Friday night and next. I wait for her to get in touch with me. She doesn't. I can't really blame her. I get a UTI. My acne goes insane, with painful cysts covering my jawline. We do not say goodbye in any form. This is astounding to me. She blocks me on Goodreads so I block her on Twitter. We will do this blocking and unblocking and following and unfollowing game more times than I can keep track of. It is the final way in which we communicate.

The night I leave, Lily and I throw my two suitcases in the back of her white truck and we drive to the airport. Each time I open my mouth to speak, I think I will cry. I want to live in the presence of Lily, in this truck, forever, driving forward. We drive past my ex-boyfriend Isaac's apartment; I see his car parked on the street. It is the car that picked me up at the airport a year earlier, when I'd shown up confused, looking for answers.

At the airport, I listen to sad songs, pretend to be in a movie.

Home. My mother and I have a movie night. We rent *Gone with the Wind* and mix M&M's and popcorn together in a bowl.

I go to lunch with an old friend. In the year I've been gone, she's also had her first experience with a woman, a girl we knew in high school. At the end of our discussion, putting our wallets away, she says, *I don't know, it was fun, I didn't overthink it.* This statement is so contrary to what I've experienced that I almost laugh. My sense of humor slowly acquainting itself with me.

The lesbian couple across the woods have broken up after twenty years. I am simultaneously unsurprised and shaken. *You never really know what's going on in other people's relationships*, my mother says. One woman has moved into the city, and the other will stay in the country. *Did they say why?* I ask. *It shouldn't be this hard to be together*, one of them told my mom. I walk the circle in the woods. We don't live more than a two-minute walk away from them. I see their huge house, their two deck chairs outside. When I return to my house, I notice a wrapped gift in the mudroom. I can tell without opening it that it's candlesticks. There's a note addressed to my mom, wishing her a Merry Christmas and a Happy New Year. It's signed from only one of the lesbians. I let myself think back to the year before, how I woke in Finn's bed on New Year's Day.

Like with any ex-lover, I sometimes find myself doing things I picked up from Finn. I say *That's bananas*, now. I drink Airborne because according to her it's better than EmergenC. I don't eat salad on its own anymore (*salad on its own is depressing*, she said). I consider the softness of the clothes before I buy. I read more Jack Spicer. I take into account the writing tip she gave me, *Never say 'very'. If you're tempted to say 'very' then you should say 'damn.'*

In the dead of winter, my mother and I drive a few hours to visit relatives. The conversation for the day turns into a gay rights discussion, because the previous day my mom and I had attended a gay wedding. We sit in the living room discussing gay politics and personal opinions. My mom says the word 'dyke' numerous times. I put none of my personal experience into the conversation, but my mom and I hold eye contact a few times, like there's a secret between us.

Driving home along the highway, I choose the album *West* by Lucinda Williams. The sky is almost black. My eyes are resting. I am trying to be good company for my mom on the three-hour drive. I am telling her about a meditation teacher I had who told us our thoughts are incredibly repetitive. That we think 90% of the same thoughts today that we thought yesterday.

Before the crash, before the smoke from the airbags, there is the sight of two deer directly in front of me. My brown eyes meet their brown eyes, their beautiful and graceful limbs bent mid-air.

Then they keep running.

There are thousands of ways to be blindsided.

Were you in love with her?

When my mother asks me this question we are standing at the kitchen counter of our house. I think I nod. I think I say, *Pshyeah*. I think I say, *I think so.* I look away from her, out the window at the large falling snowflakes. She finishes cutting a piece of silver duct tape, turns to me and sticks it over my heart, where my new down coat is ripped, the feathers coming undone, flying away, as though I have a broken wing.

ACKNOWLEDGEMENTS

Thank you for your unequivocal friendship during the writing of this book: Frances Badalamenti, Eliza Plumlee, Erika Kleinman, and Karina Briski. Thank you for your insights and eyes: Aaron Burch and Mary Miller. My parents, I am incredibly lucky to have you.

Deepest thanks to Elizabeth Ellen. I am forever grateful to your commitment to this book and companionship during the process.

Whoever is reading this, thank you for doing so.